The Jester. 11 Strange Stories

Theophilus Pomp

Published by Theophilus Pomp, 2024.

This is a work of fiction. Similarities to real people, places, or events are entirely coincidental.

THE JESTER. 11 STRANGE STORIES

First edition. June 18, 2024.

Copyright © 2024 Theophilus Pomp.

ISBN: 979-8224518630

Written by Theophilus Pomp.

Table of Contents

The Jester	1
Halos	7
The Gift Shop	13
Two for the Seesaw	33
The Wedding	37
A School Day	51
900 Miles, 9 Years, and 90 Houses	52
A Christmas Story	62
Corn	69
The First Contact	85
Ogi's Problem | $IQ_n = \Sigma IQ / [(1 + \varepsilon)n \times N0]$	87

The Jester

I sit filling the space like an idiot, rubbing my palms together, and watching how the robot tilts in front of me endlessly. I'm curious when his joints are going to give way, and it will crash to the ground like a pile of scrap metal. This will have to amuse me, and I'm going to laugh when it collapses, I'll be damned if I'm not going to amuse myself and laugh.

Motion control and reality correction.

My name is Soc Bern, and I should be incomprehensibly happy that last night's orgasm of one of the Dictors (or the Great Computer swing of mood) has made me, as of this morning, the true master of all beings and objects in the city.

„Do it, Bern!" urges and urges and roars.

Everyone admires me, envies me, adores me.

A whole pizza takes off from a waiter's tray, travels through the restaurant's window cutting out an arrowed heart on the glass, „I love you Lisa!", and stops on a policeman's hat. That's stupid. But we're all laughing, and that's fine, I have the right to defy authority. A right I've granted to myself because in an instant I could turn Mr. Uniform into a mouse and the whole town into a hot air balloon floating lazily through the afternoon sky.

This is luck, indeed, there are millions of people in the city, and only Soc Bern, for a week, the Jester. Classes are taught, scripts are sold, books are printed, all so you know how to behave when you meet the chance of a lifetime (because life doesn't have an *infinite number of weeks), all so you know how **to be** the Jester: to have fun, to perform, to be aware of and to stretch the freedom as you never have and never will.*

I get up from my chair in front of the restaurant and walk away, followed by a large group of kids, old men, loudmouths, men of honor, all laughing and pointing at me. I turn my head and smile, and their index fingers turn into crayons, they laugh happily and start drawing on their clothes.

A bus passes me slowly, the passengers giggle at me through the windows, and suddenly the vehicle softens, swells, and bursts like a birthday balloon, in the middle of the street only a huddled heap of people remain, squealing with happiness.

The sun crawls towards sunset, human organs are growing on the branches of the trees.

It's too much. I head for home.

There are some who live only for the moment when (if) they become the Jester. Soc Bern is not one of them. He didn't care. He never thought he'd get elected. And now he doesn't know if what he's doing is right. But he still doesn't care. Not of the hundreds of Jesters before him whose whims he has put up with, not of the bunch of apathetic snobs called the Board of Dictors, not of the Great Computer.

So three days pass. Blue frogs falling off from the ski, from chairs, from fences, from scaffoldings, from horses, from my own feet, from my own thoughts, croaking. I grow bored.

And again, „Doitbern!", „Doitbern!". And what now has become a chore, the inconvenience of entertaining a bunch of idiots. So many idiots.

I feel like getting drunk, I'm wondering how hard is it to find a pub where no one knows me. Hard, very hard. But I find it and shortly after I'm almost drunk. A woman sits down next to me. A prostitute, I think. I remember the store window with the arrowed heart, „I love you, Lisa". I laugh, I empty my glass and I immediately forget what I saw, what I thought, and what I remembered.

I wake up in the morning, the woman is laying next to me, naked. Skin and face tired and wrinkled, hair cut short, breasts sagging, I know how much she wants to be beautiful. To be beautiful again (or for the first time). Okay, I say to myself, then I make her look in the mirror. She squeals in amazement, she understands who I am, and obviously, now she adores me. I've fallen in love too. We kiss for a while, then I have to leave her to get down to business.

By evening all people in my city are beautiful, a few million beautiful women and a few million of good-looking men.

And that's not easy, not even for a Jester. I rest again.

What Soc Bern doesn't know is that in the end he will have to answer to the Board of Dictors and to the Great Computer for the seven days he was the true master of all beings and objects in the city. And he will receive a "Former Jester's" Merit Medal or exile.

Today I don't want to go out anymore, to see how the passers-by hurrying along the sidewalks suddenly grow roots from the soles of their shoes into the asphalt (because I want them to) and how they stumble and fall, then run away barefoot, laughing and singing. To see the tin-head robots (robot-clerk, robot-carrier, robot-janitor, robot-vagabond) crumpling like sand statues (you do this because you hate them, and that's because you can't make love to them, Freud would have told me).

THEOPHILUS POMP

I stay home and play with my neighbor's kid. I make her live multicolored bow-birds and palm-high elephants, kites, and prince-charmings. The neighbor cries, „The child has cancer". "She doesn't", I assure him, and we go on playing happily.

One-Eyed-Ben, my friend for drinking beer and ash-laden days calls me. He has lost his job. „Don't worry", I tell him, I know that after the two days I have left, there will be no more sickness and no more poverty in my town.

The last two days are torture for me, I hate to hear the crowd laughing, „Ha, ha, ha, Doitbern, Doitbern!", why the hell they don't realize the higher purpose my mission has now? I'm still forced sometimes to turn traffic lights into snakes and the snakes into strips of colored paper, to turn their hats and beanies into eggs that crack and spill on their faces.

Here comes the end, Soc Bern's day of reckoning. By tradition, a Jester should be a sad man. Why?... there's never been an answer. So he could be a jolly man. But Soc Bern was always an ordinary man. And for a week, the true master of the beings and objects of the city.

Motion control and reality correction.

The crowd chants, „Bern! Bern! Bern!", and carries me in their arms to the Dictors Seat. It seems they love me, but I have no idea, maybe this is only the ritual of sacrificing the Jester. They lift me on their palms towards the sky, and on each palm that touches me I leave a memory, it writes, impregnated matter, SOC BERN THE JESTER.

The building shaped like a mushroom (a poisonous one?) approaches us until it comes to overwhelm us with its height. Those who carried me deposit me at the entrance, and dance away. I am still a Jester, I turn the gates of the Seat into an archway of wild vines, then I go up the stairs to meet the First Dictor, now I know, to be judged.

„You have been a miserable clown and not a Jester!", he shouts at me while his glasses melt and begin to drip on his cheeks like an (I wish I'd say phlegm, it's an ugly word though, so like a:) spoonful of honey. „You were supposed to entertain people, to make them laugh, to make them cry, to humiliate yourself and humiliate them, to make them uglier and meaner. You have your sentence! The Great Computer has decided, you're doomed, exile, leave now! You are not allowed to take your whore with you! There will be no more drinking beer with Ben, no more ash-laden afternoons, no more playing with your neighbor's little girl!..." he screams. Through the open windows a cold breeze blows in, and the first stars of the night shine over the city.

It's a commonplace image, the first stars of the night shining over the city.

What people? I ask myself remembering what I had managed to forget, and what my fellow citizens had managed to forget many, many years ago, and I understand my guilt. The only human (the only human in the city? the only human in the world?) is the angry, stupid being in front of me - the First Dictor (and how beautiful is he, angry and stupid!) - and I, all of us, the inhabitants of the city, are just machines, somewhat more intelligent, more efficient, more human-like than the tin-headed-robots I hate so much. (I hate, my ass! That's how I've been programmed, all my feelings are rigged). And I, the Jester, instead of trying to randomly and infinitely complicate the social relationships...

THEOPHILUS POMP

„Agents of chaos, this is what the Jesters were meant to be, this is the only way you'll be able to recreate a society like ours", the Dictor tearfully screams, the last wish of the aging, dying species of intelligent human animals is to leave behind something that perfectly mimics it.

...I set out to make everybody the same. I hate myself, and I wish the sentiment is true.

I must prepare for exile.

Then, in a deserted place outside the city, alone, Soc Bern watches the blood oozing from his slit veins and knows he's going to die. In any case, not like a machine.

Halos

The events of this story, whose humble and fortunate witness I was, took place on a distant planet that you, dear reader, may know from the travels you have undertaken – with your body or with your mind – and in a time to which you are now either younger, older, unborn, dead or – why not? – contemporary.

It is again possible to recognize these events. Or to have lived them. You may know the characters of the story. You may know me, as I said above, the faithful and humble, the lucky and the reliable witness, and this will only reinforce the fact that all that you will read below is the actual truth, as it wanted to reveal itself to me, whose slave I have always striven to be and I will continue to be until the end, as decided by the Creator, of my life.

I shall call that planet Earth. And the sun of that planet I will call Sun. These words are of little importance because each of you will recognize in your inner self, embedded in its depths, the true names of that planet and that sun.

I arrived there on one of my space wanderings, driven by instinct and the desire to know, by the artistic nature I like to think I have, that unquenchable curiosity, that ability to feel differently from others, to rejoice at the twinkling of a star, to experience the pain of a burning meteorite and the love of all my fellow thinkers, whatever their appearance – stone, ocean, grass, bird, man or unicorn – all of which have taken me, again and again, to all corners of known time and space, to all corners of the rational, the imaginative and the subconscious and beyond, journeys which I have embedded in Memory, and I have Narrated, to justify the existence: of myself, of space and time, of the rational, the imaginative and the subconscious.

The first person I met on this planet, the stage on which the acts of this chronicle were played out, as decided by fate, by me, and by themselves, was Halos, a particularly courteous batrachian who greeted me as I disembarked from my spaceship on the platform at the top of Mount Onir. He made such a strong impression on me at first sight that even now, after so much time that has passed since then, I can't believe he's gone.

But forgive me for anticipating. His image lingers so strongly in my mind that I can hardly contain myself to write this testimony according to all the rules of art.

Halos was magnificent. His back was covered with a silky thin skin of immaculate white, and his abdomen with greenish shining scales, as big as a large palm; a human's palm, of course, for he rested resolutely and gracefully on three pairs of horny, muscular paws, finished with meticulously sharpened nails painted în yellow. The amphibian's torso and neck, if they could be called that, were unusually long, rising almost vertically to the height of a man and ending in an elongated skull adorned at the front with a surprisingly human face. From the nape of the neck to the tip of the tail, a bony, crenelated dorsal ridge flowed in a zigzag pattern, with a finger-thick golden ring hanging from the top of each triangle.

THE JESTER. 11 STRANGE STORIES

„Welcome, stranger! I am glad to see your face and feel your breath. Please taste and enjoy the hospitality of Halos, lord of Mount Onir, and of all the valleys that surround it."

Halos smiled courteously at me, his manners and words were in keeping with his appearance, and I would not have been surprised to see, if I had wounded him in some way, clear blood flowing from the cleft of his body, cold and blue as the sky of my native planet on clear winter days.

Halos's castle stood on the spot where the Mother Basin – so he confessed to me the huge lake was called, resting atop Mount Onir, a few hundred paces from the platform on which I had landed – thundered down in a magnificent crash of waters (the most awesome fall you could imagine, dear reader, being to it as the cooing of a baby to the howl of a war party), giving birth, in a terrible and eternal torment, to the River Gran. The castle made entirely of marble – white, red, black – and crystal had its foundations sunk deep into the abyss where the tumultuous sheet of water fell. From there it tore upwards through the waters and rose almost a hundred paces above the Mother Basin. On the water-submerged levels dwelt Halos, his servants and friends, fish and newts, mermaids and giant daphnia, whelks and crustaceans, multi-colored fans, claws, ribbons, tubes and braids pulsating alive in the palace's sprawling halls. And everywhere there was no furniture or decoration but sparkling mosaics of precious stones – diamonds and pearls, sapphires and rubies, emeralds, jasper, hyacinth, sardonyx and chalcedony – and columns, carvings, and bas-reliefs, all representing fantastic beauties or monstrosities of the deep. Atlases of grey granite in tortoise shells were supporting trays of greenish liquid, blinking merrily along patches of dried mud, supporting the castle vaults, the world. The portion above the water was reserved for guests like me, helpless beings of land and air.

You may wonder how I can describe these beauties so thoroughly. I will tell you that they all passed before my astonished, frightened, and charmed eyes. I agree you should be incredulous, dear reader, for I was incredulous myself when, beside Halos, stepping down on the marble steps, I descended into the waves and found that I could live in the deep as well as I did on land. The water no longer changed the color of my skin, no longer gouged my eyes out, no longer stuck out my tongue, no longer swelled my chest, no longer sucked my blood, and my life. And this was all true because you can't say that everything you're reading now is a fancy, that I never wrote these, but maybe I just thought them up in a flash before I died; that in three days' time I'll be thrown, already rotting, on the deserted bank of a river, somewhere, on a far away planet in the universe.

Yes, wonderful days I lived in Halos' unequaled palace!

There was only one thing about my host that marred the heavenly harmony and peaceful bliss of the world he cared for and ruled. Like any self-respecting batrachian, Halos breathed both in water and in air, albeit with a reduced capacity in the latter medium. And his skin, in prolonged contact with the air, began to emit vapors of substances that clouded your mind, made you dream, imagine worlds and think you were living in them, feel dizzy and gay, see what doesn't exist, and leave your own body. You know these substances, dear reader, don't you?

One day I showed Halos a jade statuette I had bought with me from my home planet, the shining nude of the Goddess I worship. I had improvised a shrine for her in the highest room of Halos's palace, she was the Sun Goddess and had to stay as close to the Sun as possible. I used the shrine to make her daily offerings and to burn myrrh, whose pleasant-smelling smoke voluptuously surrounded her calves and thighs and waist and breasts, thus uniting my faith with divinity. From the day he saw the Goddess, Halos fell in love with her. I know, it seems absurd for a batrachian prince to fall in love with a jade statuette, but the former began to climb the palace tower, on his three pairs of horny paws, more and more often, ponderously, to posternate in ecstasy for hours at time în front of the Goddess. Halos would then implore me to tell him stories about her, myths and legends; he had forgotten all about the world he had mastered until my arrival on the planet. Rarely he would roll in the Basin's crystalline waters to soak his skin dried by the heat of the Sun, whose human personification he now loved.

During one of our long talks, he confessed to me that the way he looked was the result of a spell. A witch had transformed him from an unimaginably handsome prince into a disgusting beast because he had refused her love. And that he could only return to his original condition when he loved and was loved again when a woman queen would kiss him on the lips. And that the woman he had waited for all his life was the very one I kept in the uppermost room of his palace.

I realized then that Halos had fallen prey to the pleasurable poisonous fumes his own body exuded. It was of no use to try convincing him that it was all a dream, no use for my pleas and cries. A few days later I found Halos curled up before the jade Goddess, with his lovely white skin on the back wrinkled and cracked and dry as birch bark. The noblest batrachian I had ever known had died asphyxiated.

I threw him into the water abyss for him to find his ancestors, then I set off to explore new places on the planet. I found hills and plains, mountains and oceans, cities and people. Yes, people! Like me, like you. I told them about the strange events I lived when I arrived on their planet, but no one had ever heard of Mount Onir, the Mother Basin, the River Gran, the marble and crystal palace, of my former friend and wonderful host.

At first, they thought I was a loony, but because my ship harbored many riches and far too powerful means of destruction, I persuaded some of their scholars to accompany me in an attempt to rediscover the fairytale realms I had described. And although the coordinates of all the places I had passed through were stored in the ship's electronic brain, I never managed to find Halos' palace again. Instead, I came across plenty of other wonderful happenings, inconceivable beauties, and people who also became my friends.

In truth, these latter adventures are those which I would have liked to describe in my chronicle. And I would definitelly do it if you had the time, but first, please forgive me, dear reader, for boring you with such a long and uninteresting introduction. I felt duty bound to explain what is meant by that one word which, by an incomprehensible whim of my mind, I have placed as the title of the story.

The Gift Shop

He had spent the afternoon doing what he thought it was his duty to do, what thousands and thousands before him, and thousands after him, had done, and would do again, in the little town founded almost two hundred years before by a handful of Bavarian immigrants, which had since become an insatiable tourist trap. He had entered all the souvenir shops strung along the winding alleys that made up the old center, tried on the hats and masks with Gothic motifs, giggled at the inscriptions on the always overpriced T-shirts, and ended up buying a little nothing from every one of those stores, compelled by the long, reproachful stares of the shop girls and salesmen, the patrons and shop owners. He had bought a set of glasses from the wine shop to get a free wine tasting, had been enchanted by the decorations sold at the shop called the 'Enchanted Forest', had eaten cotton candy and baked chocolate caramel apple, had spent endless minutes standing still in front of cuckoo clocks, took the mandatory boat trip on the river that divided the town into two almost equal parts, and before getting lost for the rest of the evening in one of the beer halls on the main street, decided to enter one last gift shop, the one at the end of the wooden bridge built over the river more than a hundred of years ago.

"Good evening", he smiled at the girl behind the cash register.

THEOPHILUS POMP

She smiled back at him. A little plump, she had blue eyes and looked very young, barely out of high school.

He admired the handcrafted leather goods, the hunting knives with inlaid handles, postcards racks, elegantly avoided the jewelry display case and the purses racks, pretended for a moment to be interested in the knitted scarves and sweaters, and ended up heading for the corner of the store that hid the clearance shelves.

There, lying on the carpet under the lowest shelf, he saw her: the head and the torso with only one arm twisted behind the back. He bent down and stroked her cheek lightly. It was cold. And he couldn't help but fall in love with her, as she sat, wide-eyed, dismembered, and sad, on the carpet. That had been his first thought. The second was that the bastards had used her and now planned to throw her away like a rotten apple. It was autumn, the end of the season, who knows for how long it had been sitting there, forgotten.

"Do you need help with anything?" the blue-eyed girl called, making him jump.

He banged his head against the edge of the shelf almost knocking over the heap of low-priced goods piled on top of it.

"I'm sorry, I didn't mean to frighten you," said the girl. "But, you know, we close in five minutes."

"Don't worry, it's nothing" he replied, rubbing the top of his head with the palm of his hand, "I was leaving anyway."

He got out.

It was not evening yet, but it was getting dark due to a low, grey layer of clouds that had added to the late September hour twilight. He congratulated himself that he had parked his car not far from the shop. Across the street was the beer hall that copied in atmosphere and decor, but on a much smaller scale, the Hofbrauhaus am Platzl, which he had visited some years before in Munich. "Only a beer", he thought, raising his eyes to the sky, it was quite possible that the rain would catch up with him on the drive back.

He ordered a Paulaner Oktoberfest special edition, staring insistently into the waitress's deep cleavage. She didn't seem to mind, brought him the beer rather quickly considering the number of customers in the restaurant at that hour, and smiled at him complicitly; smile and cleavage verified so many times in the past to work together as flypaper for fat tips. He stretched his legs, tired from all the walking, underneath the table, and began to take small, deliberate sips from the cold beer.

The large, gray, staring into emptiness eyes of the dismembered mannequin from the souvenir shop wouldn't give him peace. They seemed so real that in those few minutes he had spent kneeling in front of it – in front of her, it was obvious that the mannequin was, if you could call it that, a female – he expected them to blink at any moment.

He finished his beer, paid, leaving a substantial tip for the waitress, her cleavage and smile definitely worked, and crossed the street back to the souvenir shop. The next day it opened at 11 am. He looked up at the sky; it was going to rain for sure. Better not to drive at night in the rain, especially after so much fatigue gathered during the day, amplified now by the beer. He was going to call at work the next morning and let them know he was taking the day off.

He walked briskly to the downtown motel, less than a hundred yards from the beer hall. It was almost empty on a

THEOPHILUS POMP

Sunday night, at the end of the weekend; he took a random room – the cheapest – and slept soundly until morning.

It was quarter past eleven when he walked into the souvenir shop again. Behind the cash register was no longer the blue-eyed girl, but an older lady, in her fifties, perhaps the owner of the shop. He breathed a sigh of relief, he was having a vague sense of guilt, and though no one would hold him to any account, he would have felt obliged, without knowing how or why, if he were recognized, to explain why he returned.

He greeted the lady, made a completely trivial remark about the weather still being particularly nice for the end of September, and took the long way to the clearance rack.

There she was, on the carpet, motionless, wide-eyed, waiting for him.

He wandered through the discount items thrown haphazardly on the shelves, pretending not to pay attention to the mannequin. Then he raised his head glancing around, gauging the interior. He was the only customer, the older woman, the possible owner, had her back turned toward him, and was arranging postcards on a rack in the opposite corner of the store. He let his bundle of keys drop on the carpet right in front of the mannequin. He bent down and, hidden by the other shelves, and touched her face again. He ran his forefinger in a slow circular motion over the thin streaks painted with a dark bronze color on the ridge of the arches, representing the eyebrows, then around the eye socket to the temples, across the tips of the cheekbones, rested for a few seconds in the hollow between the corner of the eye and the root of the nose, and finished the motion at the midpoint between the eyebrows.

A poor, dismembered, plastic mannequin.

THE JESTER. 11 STRANGE STORIES

He retrieved his keys, got up, and headed for the cash register, grabbing something off the shelves at random: a fridge magnet with a stylized picture of the wooden bridge over the river that divided the town with, passing under it, the tourists' boat. He was in the shop for the second time and felt compelled to justify that by buying something. He took only a few steps before he felt a pair of eyes pinning him in the back of his head. He turned quickly. There was no one behind him; there was no one else in the whole store except him and the older lady. The mannequin's big, grey, still eyes pointed in a different direction. Just an impression. A few more steps and he got the same feeling of someone watching him from behind. This time he didn't stop. He took out his phone and pointing the front camera in video mode over his shoulder, tapped the recording button. He arrived at the cash register, turned off the camera, put the phone back in his left front pants pocket, paid for the souvenir, and went straight to his car.

He started the engine, put the gear in reverse, and, as he slowly backed out of the parking space, with a reflexive gesture, he reached with his left hand into his pocket to pull out the phone and throw it on the right seat. He didn't finish the gesture. He stopped the car, brought the hand still holding the phone up to his eyes, and played the few-second video clip he had recorded in the store. Although not very clear because of the up-and-down movement caused by his footsteps, the image seemed to show the mannequin's pupils moving in his direction as if following him with its eyes. Shocked, he ran the clip again, and again, and again, a few dozen times, unable to decide if what he was seeing was real or if it was his imagination

THEOPHILUS POMP

playing tricks on him, making him believe it is true what he only wished was true, until a loud honk made him flinch.

He realized he had stopped the car halfway out, perpendicular to the driveway, blocking it. He raised his hand in apology to the driver who had honked at him. He pulled back into the parking spot, turned off the engine, and went back to the gift shop.

"Excuse me," he said to the woman, "I think I lost something there" pointing to the corner where the clearance shelves were.

"Don't worry, it's alright" she replied. "No one else came in after you. What did you lose? Can I help you look?"

"A key. It came off my keychain when I dropped it earlier. But thanks, no need! I'll manage. By the way, is the shop yours?"

"Yeah, mine." (So, she was the owner!)

Then, as if trying to justify her presence there, the woman continued:

"You know, the sales are down quite a bit these days, so there's no point in paying a salesperson. In the evening, a niece comes to help me." (So the girl with the round cheeks and blue eyes...)

"Yes, I know what it's like", he said politely, although he had no idea what it meant to run a souvenir shop.

He walked over to the clearance shelves and sat down right on the carpet in front of the mannequin. Hidden by the other, taller, shelves around him, he tilted his head to one side until his gaze met the direction of the mannequin's eyes and remained like that, motionless, eye to eye for a few dozen seconds. Then he began to tilt his head very slowly, with almost imperceptible moves, left and right, up and down, trying to maintain contact. Without success, unfortunately. The mannequin's blank stare remained unmoving. The blurry video clip contained nothing. He had been dreaming.

He started to get up.

"*My name is Mira!*"

"What did you say?!" He almost cried in amazement.

The voice had been very clear, it was a feminine voice, with a pleasant timbre, but without any particular intonation, the words came out cold, like in an utterance.

"I didn't say anything, Sir!" the storekeeper replied, from behind the cash register. "Do you need help?" she asked him again, coming toward him.

"No, I don't need any help, go away! Leave me alone!" he snapped at her, then, realizing he was being rude, "Please forgive me, I'm very upset."

"I understand you are upset, maybe it was an important key. Did you find it, are you sure you don't need help?" she asked again, seeing him bent over, almost on all four, on the carpet.

"It was an important key", he replied mechanically. "Maybe I dropped it in the car", he added, getting up.

Then, suddenly:

"How much does that cost?"

That was the dismembered mannequin.

"Oh, that's not for sale..."

"Please, Ma'am, I'll pay you whatever you ask."

"I'm sorry, sir, I can't... Please understand it's not for sale..."

Then seeming to feel she owed an explanation:

"That and that one over there," she turned, pointing to a second mannequin in the shop window he hadn't noticed, "I've had them since I opened the store eighteen years ago. I found them at a flea market. I don't know how old they are, but no matter how hard I searched, I couldn't find any more like them. They bring me luck. I wouldn't give them away for anything."

She paused for a few moments as if thinking about something:

"Maybe when I'll close down the shop..."

"No problem, Ma'am, sorry for the inconvenience, and for being rude."

"I understand", she said, "perhaps it was an important key."

He headed for the exit and was only a few steps away when he heard it again.

"*My name is Mira!*"

This time, judging by the lack of reaction from the shop owner who was accompanying him, he understood that the voice had only sounded in his head. But this time he managed to suppress any reaction, went out, then stood in front of the store for a minute staring at the other mannequin in the window.

It was identical to Mira, but its torso was dressed in a white shirt with a blue blouse, looking like a traditional dirndl, on top, and had a tacky wig with blond pigtails hanging in the front, over its shoulders. It had the same fixed eyes, focused on an undefined spot on one of the rooftops across the street. Only that the gaze was devoid of any expression, he felt nothing of what had inexplicably drawn him to Mira.

He took a few steps away from the shop and, in a panic, unable to control himself, collapsed on one of the benches lining the sidewalk. He had no reason to believe that he had suddenly gone mad, he was living what social norms would call a quiet and balanced life. The stare on the back of his head, and the voice ringing in his head had to be true.

He sat there until he managed to adjust his breathing and heartbeat, thankfully the row of benches, which on other days was crowded with noisy visitors, was now empty. He got up and wandered around town for a few hours, paying no attention to the tourist traps he fell for the day before or to the people he rarely came across. He wondered aimlessly, just him and his thoughts, the still-warm breeze of early autumn and the still-green leaves of the maple trees.

Eventually, he decided to remain in the city for a few more days.

He went back to the motel, and asked for the same room, the cheapest one, until the end of the week (no, it wasn't a problem if he had to leave early, he only needed to notify the reception the day before), went to his room, and composed an email to his boss. Unfortunately, he had run out of vacation days, but a family emergency had forced him to go somewhere far away, he didn't know exactly when he'd be back, but he'd try to make it as soon as possible. The answer came almost immediately, not to worry, family is more important than anything, hope everything will be fine. If it's only a few days he'll make up for them in the future, but he should announce immediately if things change.

He breathed a sigh of relief and went out to buy a few sets of changes – undershirts, underwear, socks –, and personal hygiene items. In the morning he'd picked up a disposable razor and a disposable toothbrush from the front desk, plus a tiny tube of toothpaste, but what had started as a day trip had turned now into a longer stay.

An hour before the closing time he went again to the souvenir shop.

The girl with beautiful blue eyes was there. She recognized him:

"Welcome back, sir..."

"Paul, just call me Paul. Sir makes me feel old", he smiled.

"Angie" she replied.

"Nice to meet you, Angie!" Then: "You can't say we never tried..."

She smiled back with a slight flush in her cheeks, a sign that she knew that old cheesy song.

"I decided to stay a few more days, autumn is so beautiful here", he felt he owed an explanation. "And while I'm staying, all my friends and colleagues are going to ask me what I've brought them, so I want to spend some time at the clearance shelves, maybe I'll be able to find something for everyone."

Stupid need to keep justifying himself!

Without waiting for an answer, he went straight to the shelf and sat directly on the carpet in front of the mannequin.

"*Nice to meet you, Mira, I'm Paul*", he said, half in his mind, half muttering the words.

"*I'm Paul!*" he repeated, a little disappointed, somehow expecting Mira to answer him immediately. "*I heard you yesterday, forgive me for taking so long to come back. You know, people around me are going to think I'm crazy if they find out I'm talking to you. They think you are the leftovers of a disembodied plastic dummy. They don't know you are Mira.*"

THE JESTER. 11 STRANGE STORIES

He waited for a few minutes sitting on the floor. Mira didn't respond, the grey irises staring blankly, the coldness of the plastic making him wonder again if what he'd heard (thought he'd heard?) the day before was just a trick his imagination had played on him.

He got up and began rummaging through the shelves.

"Are you OK, Paul?" called Angie, "Should I come to help you?"

"No need, I'm almost done, thank you" he replied.

Maybe I could invite her to go together to one of the bars in town after closing, he thought, maybe I'll bring her to my motel room after that..., but instantly he felt sorry for thinking this way, the girl was almost half his age.

"*I'm cold...*" the same female voice, with pleasant timbre, but with no particular intonation, with the words strung together coldly, like in an utterance.

He looked down at the deformed head and torso, with stylized anatomical details, both naked, and an inexplicable sense of embarrassment came over him. He haphazardly grabbed a large man's t-shirt lying on the shelf, and, using it as a blanket, with his head turned sideways, but picking at Mira with the corner of his eye, like a teenager, he covered her torso.

"*Is that better?*" he asked.

The answer was not the one he expected:

"*I know you're Paul!*". Then, "*Paul just call me Paul Sir makes me feel old nice to meet you Angie you can't say we never tried are you OK Paul*", the mechanical, inflectionless repetition of the words sounded ironic and made Paul wonder if it didn't contain a hint of jealousy.

"Forgive me!" he thought/said again, *"small talk, social convenience, nothing else..."* but what if Mira could read his thoughts as well as she could read his words?

He lingered for a few more minutes and realizing Mira wasn't going to continue the conversation, he grabbed a few random items off the shelves and headed for the cash register, not before telling her:

"I'll come again tomorrow, I promise."

At the cash register, he avoided any conversation with Angie, despite her attempts and her beautiful smile.

He stopped to get something to eat at a fast food restaurant, then back at the motel he sent another message to his boss with a request for an indefinite leave of absence without pay, because of the family problems that were forcing him to remain in that faraway place.

The next morning he went again to the souvenir shop. Same explanation to Mrs. Schmidt (that's how the owner introduced herself to him):

"I've decided to stay a few more days, autumn is so beautiful here, and if I stay all my friends and colleagues will ask me what I've brought them, so I want to spend some time at the clearance shelves, maybe I'll find something for everyone."

He found the mannequin naked again, Angie had probably thought the shirt had fallen off the shelf by mistake, folded it, and put it back on the rack. He covered her again, this time without averting his eyes, the feeling of embarrassment that had gripped him the day before when he had looked at Mira with a different understanding, not like at a disembodied mannequin, was beginning to dissipate.

"I'm glad you came. I would have been very disappointed if you hadn't kept your promise. So disappointed that I don't know if I'd ever have the courage to speak to anyone from your world again."

"Why me, why me of all people?" wondered Paul.

"Because you are a good man."

Because you're a stupid man, it rang in his mind, and he immediately saddened, somehow the story of his life, the girlfriends of his youth, the wife he'd been separated from for some time now, all ended up taking advantage of his kindness.

In an outburst of anger he yanked the extra-extra-large T-shirt he had placed over Mira's torso; to punish her, to expose her nakedness, to expose her to the hulking eyes of every man who would enter the gift shop. Then he stood up and, despite her calls, *"Paul, what's wrong? Paul! Paul!"*, he walked resolutely towards the cash register.

"For a friend who's into bodybuilding", he said to Mrs. Schmidt, when she stared at the T-shirt a few sizes larger than him. Again, the stupid need to explain himself!

Late in the afternoon, after a few hours of walking around the city, enough time to calm down and realize that Mira wasn't to blame for his anger, he returned to her. They spent many minutes explaining themselves to each other, talking like two lovers, confessing and forgiving each other.

ANGIE AND MRS. SCHMIDT got used quickly to Paul's fixation on that old mannequin lying on the carpet in the corner of the store. On one hand, he didn't bother anyone at the hours when he showed up, with metronome precision, twice a day every day, just after opening and an hour before closing. The tourist flow had thinned out, it was the dead season between the early autumn and the beginning of the Christmas season. Then, they were amused by his clumsy attempts to justify his presence and, more than anything, it mattered that each time – and this was maybe another kind of justification – he bought something from the store: scarves, fridge magnets, lighters, T-shirts, mugs with local attractions inscriptions, beer mugs with Bavarian motifs, pens, plush toys...

Paul didn't realize the ridiculousness of the situation, he was happy that he had found love again, when he least expected it, in mid-life and after years of suffering through divorce and getting used to loneliness.

And what love?! In the hours they spent together, day after day, Mira told him her story: she had been born somewhere far away in the East, across many waters and many lands. She could not remember her mother, but her father had been an important man, she wasn't sure if he was the king of the whole eastern country or just a ruler of a land, or perhaps an owner of factories and lands. She remembered her happy childhood spent amongst many sisters, all of the same age and all looking the same ("*You saw my sister in the shop window, unfortunately, I lost her, they killed her soul*"). And she remembered the love and care with which a lot of people, her father's subjects, servants, or employees surrounded her and her sisters.

Then Mira told him how, one night, evil men came and kidnapped her and her sisters, separated them, and locked them in dark boxes, two by two, where they had stayed for days and nights, days and nights, days and nights until they lost their count. Then she and this sister of hers, with whom she had shared the same narrow dungeon, were given into slavery to various masters throughout the Earth until they too lost their count. Some had treated her well for a time, dressed her in expensive clothes, and brought her out to the world to be admired and adored. Then they threw her into dark, cold, damp rooms to wait for new masters. All the while she had hoped and hoped that her father's men would find her, rescue her, and take her back to her homeland. Years and years and years, without number, had passed but she had not lost hope. Unfortunately, and this had happened not long after they had both come into Mrs. Schmidt's possession, her sister had lost hope. And with her hope, she had lost her soul.

But she, Mira, had been lucky enough to keep her hope alive just a little longer (days? years? hard to say, a little longer compared to all the time that had passed since she had been kidnapped from that land to the East where she was born), just long enough to meet the good man, Paul.

And Paul promised her, swearing to her on the rest of the days he had left to live, on the sun that rose every morning and set every evening, on the ground he walked on and the air he breathed, that he would get her out of the bondage that bound her to Mrs. Schmidt, take care of her, find her father and take her back to her homeland.

And Mira replied that the father, who had certainly never stopped looking for her and her other sisters all this time, would be so happy that he would reward him as no one in the world had ever been rewarded, and, who knows, seeing that he was a good man, might even let him, Paul, be king in his place, or ruler of a land, or owner of factories and lands.

THEOPHILUS POMP

Paul begged Mrs. Schmidt a few more times to sell him the mannequin, trying to come up with more and more stupid reasons.

"Mr. Paul", she replied each time, "I've told you before, it's not for sale. I told you I've had them both since I opened the shop, they bring me luck and I wouldn't give them up for anything in the world."

One morning, it must have been about a month since Mira had first talked to him, he was about to go out for a long morning walk before eleven o'clock when the gift shop opened, he was stopped at the motel reception desk and was told that, unfortunately, his credit card had been declined. Didn't he have another one that the motel would use to hold the deposit? They tried another he gave them, but with no success.

"There must be a misunderstanding", Paul told them, "I'll call the bank today and by tomorrow it will all be sorted out", he said.

"Of course, mistakes can happen, understandably, motel management would appreciate it if they could fix it by the next day."

Paul knew what had happened: his habit of living paycheck to paycheck, alone, spending as much and as often as he wanted, with no savings, then the unpaid leave, plus the motel, food, and useless items he'd bought at the gift shop. His credit cards were probably maxed out. Overnight, he loaded the few personal belongings he had and a few blankets he'd taken from his room into the car and left the motel. He found a vacant spot not far from the gift shop and parked the car.

The next day he showed up punctually for his meeting with Mira, smiled at Mrs. Schmidt, and asked her how she was, and on his way out he bought another stuffed toy, trying to save face with the little money he had left on his credit card. But soon they were gone too. He realized he was running out of time and solutions. He slept in his car, he didn't even have any gas money left to start the engine every now and then during the night, to keep warm. The nights were getting colder and colder.

He stopped taking care of himself, unwashed, unshaven, with dirty clothes, and every day more nervous, more irritable. Several times he snapped at Mrs. Schmidt and Angie, who tried to stop him from going into the shop.

He began to shy away even from Mira, he was ashamed to stand in front of her the way he looked now. He made up reasons to cut their meetings short or postpone them.

"Why? Why? Don't you love me anymore?" she asked him seeming not to care and not to see the change.

"I do love you. I love you more than anything in the world," he replied, not knowing how to explain to her that his dream of being the prince on a white horse coming to her rescue, overcoming all the obstacles that stood in his way, was getting further and further away.

This went on until one evening when, trying to sneak into the shop, he found, to his surprise, that both Angie and Mrs. Schmidt were there, arranging goods on shelves and tables. He expected to be shooed away but neither said anything, almost pretending not to notice him. He crept to the corner with the clearance items. There he stood in shock, frozen, for a few seconds. The corner had been cleared, the shelves were empty, and Mira was gone from the carpet.

THEOPHILUS POMP

"Where is she, give her back to me, where is she??!!" he found himself screaming, shaking the shelves, trying to knock them over.

He ended up at the police station where they kept him until the next day afternoon when he was taken to the local judge who served him with a huge fine and a restraining order preventing him from entering the store again.

For a few days, he stood with his hand out, begging, in front of the Bavarian-style beer hall. He was trying to raise some gas money so he could go home. Tourists were rare, and the locals didn't visit the restaurant often. In the evening, after the souvenir shop had closed, he would prowl around the gift shop like a tired, hungry dog around the household he had been chased away from.

He saw that Mira's sister, the one with a dead soul, had also disappeared from the shop window. A few days later he saw a notice on the door that the store was closing for a week to prepare for the winter season. The glass doors and shop windows were covered with blue paper. He began to hope again. The evil Mrs. Schmidt had used Mira and now she planned to throw her away like a broken tooth. All the better for him. He postponed his return, he was convinced that this time was for the last time, and, night after night, he rummaged through the bags of garbage dumped in the dumpster behind the store. Sometimes he found fresh scraps of food which he swallowed greedily, other times he found slightly broken or worn merchandise, good stuff as well, which he collected and took to the car, you can never tell what acquaintance will ask you about the place you've been living for so long and you will realize you haven't prepared anything to give her. But he found no sign of Mira or her sister. That's okay, he had plenty of patience.

Then the day came when the store reopened for the Christmas season. That morning he woke up with difficulty, he was cold, curled up, wrapped in dirty blankets in the front seat of the car, surrounded by the pile of useless items he had bought or collected. He was hungry, but he felt too weak to go begging or rummaging through the dumpsters behind the restaurants. He closed his eyes and tried to fall asleep again. After a while, the cool glowing late autumn sun shining through the dirty windshield of the car ended up warming him, and he fell for a few hours into a state of daydreaming, fragments of reality mixed in his mind with fragments of dreams, and with disparate fragments of memories. He daydreamed himself at work, his fingers tapping on the dashboard of the car like on a keyboard, and the silhouettes of the now leafless trees glimpsed through the car's dust-covered window blending into the ones he was used to seeing through his office window. He remembered his wedding day and saw his wife – he had since separated from – in the white wedding dress, but having the color of the eyes and the blank stare of Mira. He dreamed of himself in a faraway eastern land dressed as a medieval prince surrounded by a sea of plastic mannequins. He remembered when, as a child, Santa Claus had mixed up the presents and given him a package with a giant, two feet tall doll that was meant for his little sister.

Eventually, the hunger woke him up from his lethargy. He got out of the car and headed for the Bavarian-style beer hall in the center of town, passing the now multicolored lights of the souvenir shop windows and signs. In the middle of the window, dressed in princess clothes and with a glittering tiara perched atop a wig of long, blonde hair, he recognized Mira. He remained pinned in front of the window for several minutes. She looked happy, back into the spotlight, eyes twinkling with pleasure, gaze half-smiling, contemptuous. She didn't seem to recognize him.

"Mira, Mira, it's me, Paul," he pleaded a few times, then understood: she didn't want to talk with him. She pretended not to recognize him because she didn't need him anymore.

"Bitch!" he shouted. "Stupid, ungrateful bitch, I sacrificed everything for you!"

He rushed into the store, knocking over shelves full of new merchandise, tearing down garlands of multicolored lights, trying to get to her and rip off her tiara and her princess clothes, to scoff her, and to wipe the superior smile off her face.

The judge sentenced him to six months in prison for disturbing the peace, destruction of private property, and failure to comply with a restraining order.

At the end of the day that was not too bad, at least he had a warm place to stay and enough food over the winter. Then who knows, maybe he had just misjudged her, maybe Mira behaved like that because she had fallen under the spell of the evil Mrs. Schmidt. And maybe, when he returned, he'd be able to convince her to run away with him, away from the dungeon she'd been locked in for so long, which was the gift shop.

Two for the Seesaw

The first-person narrative is so terribly dangerous sometimes.

"Look!" says the magus, and I'm not sure if his lips indeed moved, or if the evening breeze coming through the open windows fluttered his thin grey beard. Between him and me, the crystal globe is radiating so strongly that is completely overpowering the dwindling light coming from outside. The magus' scraggy fingers are coming together above the globe projecting figures on the walls, like in a Chinese shadow play. A dog. The shadow comes off the wall, gains volume, and I watch dumbfounded how it jumps and bites my hand.

I OPEN MY EYES, IT'S almost dark outside, I'm alone in my room, at my writing desk, and the evening hum of the city comes in through the open window. It hurts. I look at my hand, it's bleeding, four holes ripped in my skin and flesh stand witnesses of... Of what? I should pay a visit to my friend, the doctor, for the rabies vaccine.

Eh, what did I just tell you? Terribly dangerous! And this is not the first time when it happens to me.

I decide to quit writing for a while. I won't even read books. Simply, I will rest. And I will get wasted every night at the pub on the corner of my street. Maybe it will go away. I turn off the laptop, get up from my writing desk, lie on the couch, and fall asleep.

The next morning I don't find my car in the spot I usually park it, right in front of my apartment building, but a couple of hundred feet down the alley. Someone was in the mood for a ride last night. However, it is locked and nothing is missing inside. I don't call the police. Nothing would have happened even if I called them. I start the engine, but the car barely moves. The tires are sunk into the asphalt. The car finally breaks free, I look in the rearview mirror and I see the imprints, almost like potholes, and, behind them, finally paying attention, I realize that the asphalt is wrinkled from the place where I found the car, all the way to my regular parking spot. I'm wondering how heavy the guy who wanted to go for a ride was.

I arrive at my friend, the doctor. I ask him for the vaccine.

"A stray dog" I explain.

He doesn't seem surprised, even though there have been no stray dogs in the city for decades. He's used to my "accidents", a little out of the ordinary. He opens a container where he keeps the rabies vaccines. No vials in it. Instead, there is a solid, thin, silver layer at the bottom of the container. On top of it another layer, transparent, like a glass, covered by a clear liquid.

"What the hell?!" he says.

He raises his shoulders, shakes the container, dips his index in the liquid, tastes it, hmmm, then toward me:

"When did you talk last time with my assistant?" Then "That's OK, you don't need a vaccine, it's going to take way more than this to kill you!"

He's convinced I'm playing a trick on him (stray dogs, eh?).

THE JESTER. 11 STRANGE STORIES

I leave the office. Across the street from the medical center is a fashion store for men. I glance at the store windows and cannot control a demented laugh bursting out of me. The mannequins have grown gigantic penises ripping through their dress pants. I decide to leave the car in the medical center parking lot and go for a walk around the city. I grab a newspaper from the nearest newsstand and read that Venus of Milo in the Louvre Museum had grown arms, with the right hand raised and the middle finger pointing at the sky.

I remember my commitment to getting drunk every night. I wake up the next day with my left hand sunk into the floor all the way to the shoulder. Smashed, I fell asleep under the table and, as everybody knows me at the corner pub, they decided not to bother me. I push hard to get up and the hand comes slowly out of the floor. Two fingers are missing. Someone, something broke them like two pieces of chalk. The stubs are clean and soft. No wounds or scars. Even more shocking is that I have not written anything for two days. Not a single word. I've never even imagined something like this. The figments of others around me should not affect my reality.

In the city everything is deformed like in a movie cartoon. The people look like images in a carnival mirror. Today I saw a tree knotted twenty-three times. There is not a building, a curb, or a light pole holding itself in place.

I walk. Nothing else I can do. My laptop got a gel-like appearance. And the old typewriter I pulled from the closet has the type bars twisted and weaved together, pulsing like little flatworms.

I walk. I gave up using the car; I'm trying to save the car from having surgery later on when the transformation will be

THEOPHILUS POMP

complete (you all heard of kidney stones, didn't you?). I'm only wondering if tomorrow I will wake up again, or I will become a lifeless object who will remain like this for millions of years until the seesaw will flip and we'll become living matter again.

And I'm asking myself, what piece of plastic from the garbage container behind my apartment building I should inform (very important, my friends!) how terribly dangerous is the first-person narrative.

The Wedding

„A pair of skunks, I watched them from my bedroom window as they moved, it was like a ritual dance, like a wedding... a skunk wedding on my back lawn". Damn that Alex, he was the only one of our group who owned a house and he never missed an opportunity to brag about it.

Alex had been in – or worked for – the Russian army, something to do with missiles, he designed or built them, (or just guarded them, the Greek thought) and he had been kicked out (or run away), and now he was trying to keep as low a profile as possible, and make the most of the chance he'd been given to start a new life.

I didn't quite know how to read Alex's stories, either he was a master of dissimulation who played a perfect act, or (as the Greek thought) he liked to brag about things, but he wasn't smart enough to make it believable.

„I don't remember how long the dance lasted, maybe a quarter of an hour, maybe more, but I felt so happy watching them, I wished it would never end. Then, from among the thuja bushes that mark the boundary between my backyard and my neighbor's, four kits appeared, one after the other.

„This is no longer a wedding, it's a christening!" said the Greek.

The Greek thought Alex's stories were silly, we spent almost every break at work listening to either what Alex had dreamt the night before, as in this case, or to his lectures on extinct species, climate change, and the end of the world. They sounded just as silly to me, but along with Frank's crazy business ideas and Big Sam's jokes, they helped to save us from the loneliness lurching inside ourselves for twenty minutes, twice a day, every day. The only one who didn't seem bothered by the Russian's stories was Tony-The-Government-Will-Take-Care-Of-It.

The Greek was born in Cyprus, and was one of the few hundred survivors of the genocide. He was seven years old when, hiding in a closet, he had seen his parents shot. Then he had managed to somehow run away and sneak onto a boat, and only by great luck – or the will of God – the boat was found a couple of weeks later in the middle of the Mediterranean, floatin astray with the child almost dead, by an Italian fishing ship. He was then brought here and given up for adoption by a religious organisation.

Decades ago, the extermination of the Greek Cypriots had been one of the main subjects of the diplomatic theatre, transformed by the media and the chancelleries of the major powers into a kind of world drama. But now no one talked about it anymore – not even the Greek liked to remember that – and sometimes it's good to let things be forgotten.

„Maybe it's a wedding and a christening at the same time. It's possible that in skunks world the act of procreation is sometimes consumed outside the holy institution of marriage. Don't you, Christians, do the same?" Big Sam's voice sounded as earnest as a funeral home salesman's, not a muscle twitching on his face, only his eyes had that playful twinkle we'd all learned to recognize (all except Tony).

THE JESTER. 11 STRANGE STORIES

Big Sam was a mountain of a man with a mountain of a soul, he'd give away everything he had to help you in your time of need, God's bread is how we use to call this kind of people back in my country (Allah's bread would be more truthful in Sam's case). He worked hard to provide for his wife and four kids, and he was the only one of us who dreamed of doing something else, of moving up, maybe becoming a team lead or, why not, even getting to work in the office.

„The government will take care of it!" grunted Tony through his teeth, visibly annoyed by Big Sam's comment. As usual, Tony was the only one who didn't get that it was a joke.

Tony was what you'd call the team's fool, he broke almost everything he touched and as a result he was only asked to do the simplest of the jobs, which was always completely nothing. He was also the one with the highest seniority, no one knew when or who had hired him, let alone why he hadn't already been fired. Besides, we were all convinced that Tony would continue to be here, doing nothing, long after each of us was long gone.

Superimposed over Tony's grunt came the siren that marked the end of the break. This was the second break of the day; three more hours of silent work, then, also in silence, and in order, we would put our tools back into their places, and leave for the worries that awaited each of us outside.

MORNING AFTER MORNING, thousands of people entered the revolving gates bound by high fences made of wrought-iron bars and wire mesh, followed the paths marked with yellow paint on the large concrete plateau that surrounded the bays, were swallowed up by the conglomeration of buildings – each person by its designated door – and were scattered through the maze of corridors, tunnels, stairwells and halls. I was beginning to recognize a few of those people by sight, but I had never exchanged a word with any of them. We were bound to silence. By the contract everubody had signed, we were allowed only forty minutes of words a day, and only between those who shared the same work station. Our comings and goings resembled a silent procession, accompanied by the creaking of the cast iron gates, the thundering of the steel-toe boots and the cadenced harrumphing of the escalators.

In the case of me and my other five teammates, the maze ended in a room with white walls and a cement floor covered with grey linoleum, containing seven tall metal lockers where we kept our overalls and other personal belongings, several tool cabinets and a round metalic table surrounded by a circular bench with enough room for seven adults, both set directly into the cement floor. The room was a sort of antechamber, cloakroom and dining room at the same time. On one side, separated by a simple, windowless door, were the toilet and the showers, and on the opposite side of the entrance was an opaque, sliding panel which opened with the sound of the siren to allow access to or from our work station.

Day after day, seen from the inside, the workplace looked almost always the same: a horizontally laied metal cylinder, nearly hundred feet long, some eight and a half or nine feet high, painted green, studded at equal distances along and around its circumference with frames and I-beams, with seemingly temporary wooden platforms raised on each side and electric lanterns - also temporary - brightly illuminating every square inch of the cylinder's surface. At the ends of the structure the light ended abruptly, as if swallowed by something, the bases of the cylinder being hidden in a dense darkness.

No one knew what layed beyond the beginning of the darkness, solid walls or force fields. The subject was taboo, we had signed that we would never try to find out, just as we had for the silent comings and goings. Moreover, the Greek, whose seniority with the company – we'd heard – was even longer than Tony's, but with different teams (and every time you change teams the company erases part of your memory), had once told us a story about a kid hired right out of highschool who, while still on probation, forgot what had happened to the curious cat and stuck a screwdriver into the curtain of darkness at the end of the cylinder. The screwdriver was thrown from his hand with a force that nearly broke his wrist (force field, then!) and immediately the opaque panels opened, and two company security officers appeared out of nowhere to frame and escort him out. The Greek had been unwilling or unable to tell us what happened next with the curious young man – too many years had passed since then and he'd forgotten, or it was possible this was one of the memories the company erased – but to everyone's surprise Tony had been very vehement in claiming that the story was made up, that only in the Greek's sick mind would someone – especially someone on probation – have dared to break the rules.

Strung across the wooden platforms were white bundles of conductors and cables, some of them as thick as Big Sam's wrist, made up of hundreds of wires, long as from one end of

THEOPHILUS POMP

the cylinder to the other. Day after day, our job was to unravel bundles one by one, install them along the metal structures and connect them together in prearranged patterns; day after day, like spiders hidden from other people eyes, we wrapped the green cylinder in a white web of copper and plastic.

The differences from day to day were too small or repeated too many times to be noticed: sometimes the green cylinder was a few steps longer or a few steps shorter; sometimes the metal structure was slightly altered dictating different connections between cables, sometimes a bundle of wires had to be separated or a conductor added or removed from the web.

„HEY, MR. COLLEGE DEGREE, take a look at these and tell me what you think!"

College Degree was my nickname, this because I made the mistake to tell everybody that back in my home country I had a college degree, that nobody cared about here, and *these* was another one of Frank's little financial tricks, one of those that were supposed to get us out of the slavery of everyday work, to make us rich beyond imagination - both us and our children, and our children's children.

First of Frank's businesses to which he had all of us chipping in with some dough, some two or three years ago, was the trade with ceramic garden gnomes imported from Eastern Europe. He had brought in several hundred dwarfs that he had originally stored in a leased warehouse space. After a while, after we run out of money for rent, he moved them with him into his apartment. At first it was tough, but then he got used to it: rows after rows of garden gnomes lined up on the shelves

THE JESTER. 11 STRANGE STORIES

Frank had covered his home walls with, gnomes in closets, gnomes in cupboards and kitchen cabinets, ceramic gnomes under tables, on windowsills and along the beds. He gave each of them a name, which he then learned by heart. When he managed to sell one, he'd cry for days at a time as if he'd lost his own child, then came and showed us with well documented figures how close we were to recouping our investment. (We were not close!)

The paper Frank handed me had small numbers written in three columns on both sides, numbers that looked like lottery combinations.

„So?" he said impatiently.

„So what?"

„A friend gave them to me. He's been working on this scheme for two years. 95% guaranteed to win the jackpot."

„It doesn't look like any scheme, it looks like random numbers. With all the combinations written here, the chance is about one in three million. Why isn't he playing these numbers?"

„It's a scheme! He says he's already checked it for the last two months, week after week. But he doesn't have the money to play all the combinations..."

„And he gave them to you for free, like a fool?" Alex asked.

„It's not really for free, he wants 10% of the winnings... like a fool. Are you in?

A long silence, then the Greek:

„I say let's get in! Even if we don't win, it's not big loss. On the other hand, if the government wants to sell the company to the Russians, most of us will probably be kicked out..."

Then looking straight at Alex:

„...except for those who, în the past, might have been part of the *raketnye voyska*".

„Those are the ones likely to be promoted!" continued Big Sam earnestly, catching the Greek's remark on the fly.

„The Government will take care of it", said Tony, and I could have sworn a playful smile twitched in the corner of his usually opaque eyes.

Unfortunately we missed Alex's reaction because immediately the siren that marked the end of the break sent us all back to work.

THE SEVENTH IN OUR team was Rafael, the team leader. One day, two or three weeks ago, he came from a meeting with the supervisor (that was the team leader's advantage, in addition to the forty minutes of words a day, he got another twenty minutes a week of talks with the supervisor) and told us to slow down a bit, just enough to force some overtime, but careful not to let the office bosses realize (we got overtime when we couldn't complete installing all that wiring during regular work hours). This was to put a little extra money in our pockets. Once because the work was getting incresingly complex, and the number of mods we had to do was higher and higher, then that there was no telling what was going to happen in the future. This top-secret project we were working on was too big for one company, maybe even for one country. Already the cylinders we were stuffing with the white spider webs made of plastic and copper were coming from China, and it seemed that other governments, from Latin America all the way to Russia, were becoming interested in taking on a share in the project. I don't know if the supervisor had been drunk when he told Rafael all these, but the fact is that from the next day on our foreman stopped showing up for work. He had officially gone on sick leave, but I think someone was actually listening to the microphones hidden in the antechamber-dressing-dining-room. Or there really was a reason Tony never got fired, no matter how many things we managed to screw up.

„MY GUESS IS THAT THESE are pieces of guts built for transplant banks, and what we (who aren't humans, but nanobots programed to think they are walking on two legs) are installing aren't wires, but nerves", the Greek thought.

We were back at work, the scheme guaranteed by Franc's buddy to get us (and our children, and our children's children's children) out of the slavery, as expected, hadn't worked.

One of the favourite topics that came up from time to time in the discussions around the lunch table was trying to guess, taking turns, what the green cylinders we were working on (and in) really were... and what was beyond their dark endings.

"Train cars," Franc proposed, an idea rejected almost immediately, who the hell had ever seen round, windowless train cars before.

"Chunks of tunnels through which the train cars would run" had developed Big Sam the idea. Plausible, but why so many wires? And what need did the tunnel have for metal casing?

"Huge motor stators," I tried my luck.

THEOPHILUS POMP

"Thanks God you are the smart one, College Degree boy, we'd be lost without you!" replied the Greek. „Where are the giant poles of the giant motor stators?"

"Rockets", didn't miss Alex the opportunity to show off, although someone who had actually designed or built (or only guarded) rockets would have known that their structure should be quite different.

"Airplanes," said Tony out of the blue.

"Even the crocodile flies, but not too high" I retorted and only the end-of-break siren managed to stop the roars of the others rolling on the grey linoleum with laughter.

THIS TIME, AS SOON as the Greek opened the discussion, we all sensed something was amiss. Big Sam's face was covered with shadows, and the almost everlasting smile at the corners of his mouth was gone.

„Tony, swear on the life of your children that everything we'll talk about now stays between us", he said.

„What the hell, man?" Tony tried to protest, but Sam's frown (and as big as Sam was, frown was downright fierce) stopped him.

„I swear", Tony whispered.

„I think I know what we're building: an elevator well. A space elevator well."

Five drooping jaws, five pairs of eyes staring in disbelief.

„It starts in China, and because it needs to be well anchored it tunnels through part of the Earth's crust, then emerges directly perpendicular to the surface and extends, pushed tube after tube after tube, towards the moon. We work somewhere just below the surface, at base of the elevator well."

On any other day it would have been obvious he's making fun of us. Now we listened to him in silence unable to decipher whether Sam was outright mad or whether what he was saying contained even a glimmer of truth.

„Well, if you say the tubes are perpendicular to the Earth surface, how can we stand up straight in them?" asked Franc.

„Artificial gravity. Just because we can't feel the difference it doesn't mean it's not true. The senses are easily deceived. Have you ever wondered why the many corridors and staircases leading here, to our work place, are so long? Haven't they always seemed too long to you? Maybe they're not "too long", but just long enough for the perspective to be modified and the change to be imperceptible. Plus polarized light, holograms and mirrors so nobody could see the elevator above the ground level aiming for the Moon. Have you ever noticed there are no airplanes and no birds flying over our bays?"

„The government will take care of it", added Tony, and no one felt the need to mock him.

Then silence until the end of the break and silence again until the end of the working day.

———◉———

A FEW DAYS PASSED WAITING in fear for the consequences. Work, home, work, home, with nothing out of the ordinary happening, it seemed that this time the guy who should have been listening to the microphones planted in our team's anteroom the day Sam had shocked us with his theory had fallen asleep with the headphones on. Or maybe he had diarrhea and spent most of his time on the crapper. Or Tony had kept his promise.

I remembered reading in the official media a few years back about some of the world's crackpot billionaires wanting to build an elevator to the moon, but the whole thing had seemed too far-fetched to pay any attention to. And now there was a slim chance that my own hands had been helping to build it.

It was hard to contain our thoughts. On one side was China – the only country left in the world where you could live without being a slave to consumption society, and over which no other government had any influence, on the other side was the endless potential of space – beyond the satellites belt the space colonisation was beginning, and out there the laws of nations no longer applied. And here we were, suspended near the middle of the umbilical cord bounded at both ends, with freedom.

„HOW FAR DOWN DO YOU think the Chinese are?" Tony asked.

„I don't think they're very far. If all these tubes are coming from them, somewhere right under these buildings there must be something like a customs house where our government takes them in... then China as far as the eye can see". The twinkle in Franc's eyes meant that the wheels in his brain were already in motion seraching for a new deal.

„There is only one way to find out" the Greek said mysteriously.

???...

THE JESTER. 11 STRANGE STORIES

„College Degree, he said, all the several thousand employees of the company come at the same time, leave at the same time".

„Except for those who work overtime!" I replied.

„Right, but the siren still goes off for everyone at the same time and those who stay back take breaks at the same time. Is that right?"

The question was rhetorical, a slight nod was enough.

„Do the math, then, how much energy does it take to get all the sirens to sound and all the sliding panels to move at the same time?"

„Assuming all employees' jobs are similar enough..."

„What would you do then, throw a bunch of extra money into the electrical distribution system to make it able to withstand the power spike that happens only few times a day, or shut off the power to other systems that aren't needed when the sirens sound and the sliding panels slide? And what is the system that normally burns a lot of power, but to which everyone turns their back when they line up at the door? The system that no one thinks about, because everyone is just anxiuos to leave this damn shitty place? The system we all signed up to never even get close to it?"

„Which system?" asked Tony, but no one answered him, by now we had all become less talkative.

Overlaid on the silence was the siren that marked the end of the break. It was the second break of the day, three hours of work left.

The next siren found us lined up at the exit from the tube with the toolboxes in our hands. We had been hard at work finishing installing the spider web of wires during regular hours, driven by the desire to get away from the place as quickly and as far as possible. Always first in front of the sliding panels was Tony, then the Greek, Frank, Big Sam, me and, always the last one, seemingly with the intention that whatever unknown dangers lurked ahead, he would leave the others to face them first, Alex.

Marking the end of the siren, over the hiss of the sliding panels, we heard a thunderclap, something heavy struck the wooden platform just behind us. It was the toolbox Alex had let go of his hand. We turned our heads, and frozen in front of the the exit, we watched him turn and set off with calculated, unhurried steps towards the patch of darkness that marked one of the ends of the green cylinder. He reached it, and with a natural gesture raised his hand and pushed. The hand passed through it without resistance. He stepped forward and was swallowed by the darkness. And immediately a series of quick rattles in the wooden platform told us that Alex had broken into a run.

We listened for a while in a mixture of astonishment, envy and joy – look at this damn Alex! and we who always thought of him a coward beyond compare... – until the sound of footsteps trotting on the platform gradually faded into the distance.

Then coming from far away, barely perceptible, there was a short bang, like the slamming of a door, perhaps the door that marked the beginning of freedom. And only the Greek – the only one who had the right to claim that he had ever heard such a noise before – could have sworn that what we all heard was the sound of a gunshot.

A School Day

First, they had Biology. The teacher came naked...
"Grosss!!!" shuddered Mary, seeing his stainless steel skin,
...And began explaining: his head, members, heart, lungs, and the other internal organs came apart from his body, floating through the classroom from student to student.

Second came Math. Johnny, a cute little boy with blond hair got lost in a dissertation on the Möbius strip. Although this had only one side, nobody could find him again.

Next class – Writing – they rolled a pile of zeros and ones back and forth through the classroom until they succeeded in arranging them into something called a story: "once upon a time..."

The visual arts were next. The teacher:
"Children, who want to help me?"
"Me", said Anne-the-freckled, and the other students connected their minds to hers, and shaped her into a bird, then in a sunset, in the thinker, and in whistler's mother.

When the bell rang at the end of the school day, in the classroom stepped Mom, a *woman*, who took apart and arranged neatly in boxes the teacher and the students except one who grabbed her hand and went home together.

900 Miles, 9 Years, and 90 Houses

to C.G.

THE DISTANCE THAT SEPARATES me from my old friends I measure in hundreds – in some cases thousands – of miles, and in the number of years that passed since I last saw them.

I remember, for example, my last meeting with Ycalin, shortly after the war began. We had each traveled about half of the 900 miles that separated us, to see each other.

"Maybe for the last time," he said.

Then, I hated him for saying it. For daring to say out loud what was also in my mind, but I refused to believe. I wish I could continue to refuse to believe it now. Nine years have passed, the war shows no sign of ever ending, and I no longer have enough courage to continue refusing to believe.

I get up from my chair, take a few steps across the room to stretch my legs, and glance through the window behind the computer screen, over the basil plants growing in the pot on the corner of my desk. The neighbor across the street is tending the lawn. He's in his eighties – how many wars has he survived? - and with all the craziness that surrounds us, he acts as if lawn care is the most important thing in the world. As if the list of preparations for the end of the world included the obligation to find not a speck of weed or dandelion in his front lawn.

THE JESTER. 11 STRANGE STORIES

I look at my watch: one minute and twenty four seconds to go before his allotted time expires. He slowly gathers his gardening tools, looks long and hard, left and right, at the deserted street, admires the lawn for a few seconds, then looks up at the window under the cornice of the house across the street. That's where I am. Our eyes meet for a split second. Though from down there he can't see me through the window I'm sure he knows I'm watching him, and exactly five seconds before his time is up he enters the house.

I go back to work in front of my computer, I've been working from home since the war started, happy to have managed to keep my job, there are so many others who have lost it and been thrown into poverty and deprivation, now living of the mercy (some would say on the debt) of the government. There are also so many others who have perished in the war, and those left have had to make the sacrifice of working harder and harder. We went from eight to ten, and now to twelve hours a day. I have almost two hours left until my next break and then three more until the end of today's schedule.

I plan my breaks to overlap with the times when the neighbors are allowed out of their houses. The next break is in fact made up of two smaller ones: the first when the short, fat, in her late sixties or so, woman, that lived in the tower house at the end of the street, was going to parade at a brisk pace, in a white dress with orange stripes, with her peke in a short lesh, from right to left, on the sidewalk across from my house; the second small break, ten minutes later, when she would pass back, this time at a much slower pace, from left to right on the same the sidewalk across the street.

THEOPHILUS POMP

Same ritual: I get up from my chair, lie down on the hard floor to stretch, feel my bones creak, then I stand up, a few steps across the room, and glance out the window over the basil bush. The woman doesn't look up, always stares just straight ahead, occasionally tugging at the dog's leash, as if the rest of the world doesn't exist for her.

There are ninety houses on my street, forty-five on each side, shaded from place to place by huge oak and maple trees. The houses are made of red bricks, some single-story, with roofs with rounded cornices that make them look like the little houses from fairy and leprechaun stories, others tall, two-story, piercing the sky with sharp Tudor-style ridges. I had moved into the neighborhood only a year before the war began, and I had never exchanged more than a few hurried greetings with no more than six or seven of the families on my street.

Curiously, except for the two young sisters who lived in the house with a big porch to the left of my house, and who left to live in the country with their parents just after the war began, these six or seven neighbors were the same ones I've been seeing every day, day after day, for almost nine years from my window, coming out and going back into their houses at set times, according to the schedule created by the authorities.

The enemy (we had all forgotten whether the war was external or internal, we had also forgotten who the enemy was: the Russians, the Chinese, Arab terrorists, left-wing or right-wing extremists, aliens, ...) was cruel, ruthless, unscrupulous. It respected none of the rules of war. It seemed that its aim was to kill innocent people; as many innocent people as possible, young or old, rich or poor, children or grown men, women or men, without exception. The enemy had developed a technology, probably based on infrared rays, that detected population clusters, detected the heat of human bodies, and attacked there first, with a speed and precision that is hard to explain.

The weapon used to kill was also terrible, as the official communiqués described it, without much further detail. There was nothing of what history had taught us about armed conflict, at first we found it hard to believe that we were living through a war, there were no explosions, no destruction, no fires, no blood, no bodies torn apart, just announcements of mounting fatalities, images of rows and rows of dead bodies piled up in hospitals, morgues, crematoria, mass graves. And the continuous, deafening sound of the sirens of official vehicles: ambulances, fire engines, police, and army vehicles.

Many, too many, perished at first until the smart people in the army and the intelligence services understood the enemy's technology, and the government instituted a containment order and forbade people to leave their homes. The necessary supplies were delivered to everyone's door by infrared-shielded vans. This had saved a lot of lives, indeed, but after a year the number of suicides caused by depression among those locked behind thier own doors had exceeded the number of war casualties. Then the government decided to give everyone thirty minutes a day in which to go out, at predetermined times and on predetermined routes, decided by special algorithms that kept the infrared radiation density per unit area below a certain threshold equivalent to a near-zero risk of enemy attack.

Now, only very seldom you could hear a siren, a sign that some bastard had decided to disregard the containment order and the enemy had come for him. Both he, the idiot, and the innocent who happened to be, obediently, on the street at the same time and close enough that the infrared radiation on the surface unit would trigger the enemy's sensors. But even then the sound was coming from far away, far enough to give us a sense of security. We were almost getting used to it. Except that, just a few years ago, an incident happened that cut off both me and - it seemed - all my neighbors from any thought of breaking the authorities' orders. A group of teenagers - that beautiful and dangerous age of recklessness - had gathered, disregarding the rules, in the playground at the west end of my street, to play basketball. I didn't know these details until I saw the news reports that evening. But I heard the sirens of the fire trucks, so shrill and so close that it seemed to tear my insides apart, then, sticking my head out as far as I could through the open window - also a violation of the rules, but small, small enough to escape unnoticed and unpunished - I saw the multi-colored lights of police, fire, rescue, and military cars surrounding the little square. On the news I also saw the faces of the six teenagers who had been killed by the enemy, serene, still smiling, reflecting that stupid carelessness of their age.

I manage to pull myself out of my reverie and focus back on work. Good thing my laptop camera can't read my thoughts (at least I think so). It needs to be turned on to allow the company to verify that I'm here, in front of the screen, working, but it can't detect whether my mind is connected to the drawings on the screen. At least I think it can't.

Two hours and forty-five minutes later I log out from the account, shut down the computer, and go outside. It is my time,

THE JESTER. 11 STRANGE STORIES

I have thirty minutes in which I can experience a relative sense of freedom. I use half the time to mow the grass in front of the house, even though it's after 8 pm, it is summer and, still, plenty of light outside (and fortunately, my yard is much smaller than my neighbor's across the street), another five minutes to pull weeds out of the flower beds in the front yard, and the last ten minutes to walk from one end of the street to the other. Walking as slow as I can, I stop in front of each of the other eighty-nine houses on my street and, staring into their windows, I bow my head slightly as if in greeting someone. Although I don't see them, I know that most of the neighbors are watching me from behind closed windows, and drawn curtains, blinds, and shutters, and return my greeting.

I rush into the house seconds before time runs out, eat something even though I have no appetite, and fall asleep with a book on my chest, an easy book with a silly action whose only merit is that the events described there take place before the war.

In the morning, the first break isn't even officially a "break", because it comes just after eight o'clock, which is the start of my workday (well, as I used to say in college, anything well done starts with a break!). I don't lie down to creak my bones, I don't walk across the room, I just get up glancing out the window. The neighbor who lives three houses to my right, Eva, is doing her running schedule. Past her prime, close to my age but in excellent shape (I can't tell you what a belly I've grown since the war started), she passes by the window a few times. I like to watch her from behind, admiring her long, slender legs and her hard buttocks swaying on the rhythm of the run.

THEOPHILUS POMP

Then, at 10 o'clock, it's the other neighbor across the street, to the left of the lawn guy, turn. He is repairing, for the umpteenth time, the steps of the house's front entrance. He was the first one I met when I moved into the neighborhood. He saw me struggling to carry the furniture into the house and came to help me.

At noon, the neighbor to my right comes out with a water hose to water the lawn, the flower bed in front of the house, and his two-year-old grandson, who squeaks running around like a whirligig. They both look like they're having such a good time, but there's a look of distress in the neighbor's eyes. Before the war, he had a construction business, and now he is one of those living on the government's mercy. Others have gotten used to it, some really like it. My neighbor is suffering. The child is small, small enough that the radiation emitted by the warmth of his body makes no difference on the enemy's infrared detectors.

I don't know why I remembered Ycalin yesterday. I hadn't spoken to him in about three years, and that's when he told me about his research, that he was scouring the internet far and wide for evidence. „What kind of evidence?" I asked him. He looked at me like I'd fallen off the moon. „Evidence that war doesn't exist.". „Ha!" I then wondered if I should be worried, if the isolation had affected his uppermost organ, but I said nothing. After all, it was something to do for him. After all, he had strange ideas before and they passed.

I also don't know why I was so pessimistic yesterday. The greetings of the neighbors watching me from behind closed windows, and drawn curtains, blinds, and shutters, the impeccable lawn of the neighbour across the street, the sparkling cleanliness of white orange-striped dress of the peke owner, the happy squeak of the child, Eva's long, slender legs and hard buttocks, all these give me the strength to believe that the war will be over at some point and that I will have the chance to travel again half of the 900 miles that separate us and tell Ycalin he was wrong.

I look at my watch. Two minutes to go before the neighbor across the road comes out to tend to the lawn. I get up and start pacing the room stretching my strained back. I hear a muffled sound, a barely audible beep. A notification on my personal phone. It's Ycalin on the messaging app (what a coincidence!):

"Get out now! All is just an illusion..."

"Are you crazy?" I reply.

"GET OUT NOW!!!"

Then:

"I don't have time to explain... they will be here soon. GET OUT!!! NOW!!!"

Then his status changes to offline.

I rush like crazy down the stairs to the ground floor and out the front door. Across the street, there's no sign of the neighbor. And the lawn... The lawn!!! The grass is about a foot high, full of weeds, dandelions, thistles, and wildflowers. The house on the right has the front door broken, torn off its hinges, and a few of the windows broken as well. I take a few steps back and forth on the street, shaking like a madman. All the houses, with one or two exceptions, look like they haven't been lived in for months or maybe years. What the hell is going on?! I realize that the break is almost over and I run back into the house so I won't be late for work, so the laptop camera won't detect - report - that I am late. I collapse panting into the ergonomic chair in front of the screen.

What the hell is going on? What does he mean by all is an illusion? Is what I've just seen an illusion or the illusion is what I have been seeing every day, month after month, year after year through the window, and on my daily walk? An illusion, i.e. a hologram, or just images subliminally injected through the computer screen during the twelve hours I sit in front of it every day? Could this be an explanation of why I always see the same six or seven people: easier to build and maintain the illusion, based on the well-defined images from memory, without the risk of using the wrong characters that could have introduced suspicion? And me. who thought the monitoring system on the company laptop couldn't read minds!

Could Ycalin be right ("War doesn't exist"...)? And everything - EVERYTHING! - is nothing but a fantasy created by... By whom? And what for? And where are the others, why are there only a few, very few of us left? Are we more useful? Useful to whom? Useful how? And what happens to those who, although useful – like me -, have learned the truth?

I feel like I'm going crazy. Maybe I'm just tired and imagining things. Too many, too long working days, too similar to each other, nine years of war, nine years away from people. Maybe I'm just sick.

I hear a siren in the distance, it sounds like an ambulance, somehow the sound cheers me up, and reassures me, then it gets louder and louder. There are actually more cars with multicolored lights approaching, entering my street and blocking it at both ends.

THE JESTER. 11 STRANGE STORIES

The deafening sound of sirens is now so shrill and so close that it seems to tear my insides apart, then one of the cars stops in front of my house. I'm scared, I'm shitless scared, and I don't know why. For me the war is over.

A Christmas Story

One day Dad came from Work (I don't know who *Work* is, maybe someone who lives *outside*, I only know that every morning he says "I go to Work"), and the sleeve of his best coverall was ripped, and from his arm was dripping a red, thick liquid, and he said:

"Those damn trees"...

Plus a few other words that made Mom say:

"You should be ashamed! The boy is here!"

I understood I was not supposed to hear those words, and in fact I think I didn't hear them because I was busy watching "Bambi-Against-the-Giant-Scarab", wondering in the same time what "those damn trees" were; even if you dared me to tell you those words now, I would definitely not remember them.

Dad pulled the jacks from my head, Bambi-Climbing-a-Skyscraper became the *Home* – the place where I've been living since I was born ("You were *born* here", this is what Mom says), and said (Dad):

"Hey, *Oldman*!" (No, my name is not Oldman, but he liked calling me like this).

He had no idea that I had a *system* made in my mind I used to see Bambi and, in the same time, know what's around me. Nobody knew that, except the Little Girl. Actually she taught me how to make this system. I will tell you later who the Little Girl is.

I asked him:

"What's this?" and I touched his arm.

He winced, and replied:

"Blood. I am hurt, and I'm in pain."

I didn't know exactly what *hurt* and *pain* were, but I realized it should have been something like when Bambi-Is-Cut-In-Pieces-by-the-Bad-Coyote, or when Indians-Are-Skinning-Bambi and Bambi's inner shell is all red with some white signs looking like this: .

Then Dad said:

"Go to *Yourroom* and play!"

(Yourroom is a part of the Home).

I went, but from there I could hear him telling Mom how those damn trees invaded overnight all the streets from the old downtown, breaking the asphalt and damaging the buildings, and how his team fought the entire day to destroy them, and how he got his arm wounded in the fight. Then I realized that Dad was *brave* and a *hero* (this is how were called those who, in the spaceship movies I was sometimes watching when I got bored of Bambi, were-defending-the-Earth-against-the-Aliens-who-wanted-to-obliterate-us), and I began to hate the damn trees.

That was a wonderful day for me. Because that day I learned that my father is brave and a hero, and that somewhere outside, beyond the city, some damn trees were living. And it was also then when I found a new feeling, called – I was sure about that – hate.

Before that, every day I was watching Bambi-and-other-movies, eating when Mom called *dinnerisready*, playing or sleeping in Yourroom, and – once in a while – going by myself to that place in the home called *tothebath*. (This is how Mom called it when I was very little and I was going there together with her).

You could say this is totally boring, but I enjoyed it, plus that once a year we had the Event. A guy would come Home with a bunch of equipment, put some kind of helmet (looking like the one from Bambi-Made-Scrap-Metal-out-of-the-Viking-Android) on my head, and while shiny balls were spinning behind my forehead and between my temples, a bunch of lights would blink on the screen of the equipment. Then the guy would shake his head, and Dad would give me a sad look, and caress my forehead saying "Unfortunately, you are not allowed to go out for another year". This didn't seem too sad to me, I didn't even wanted to go out, because *out* was a frightening place, definitely full of monsters (it was for a good reason Mom was saying when she got mad at me: "Be good, otherwise I will kick you *out*!").

From the day when Dad came home wounded, I kept asking myself what the damn trees were.

I asked the Little Girl too. Neither she knew. But I promised I will tell you who the Little Girl is. One day, some time ago, when the sign which Dad draws once a year before the Event on the door frame, pressing a pencil horizontally on top of my head, was at the same level with the door knob, I felt some strange, foreign thoughts in my head. I yelled: "Who are you?" They said they were the thoughts of a little girl who lived together with her Parents in a Home on the other side of the Wall, a girl who has never been outside. Just like me. At first it was very hard for me to believe there were another Home, and other Parents, and I thought that everything was just Bambi's trick, like in Bambi-Fooled-the-Ninja-Robots. But, in time, she taught me how to send my thoughts into her mind, through the Wall, and since then we had been communicating almost all the time. We had been sharing *Experiences*. (And this was our biggest secret).

The one who shaded the light on the mystery, when I finally dared to ask her, was Mom.

"The trees? Green, giant monsters that live directly on the ground."

(How gross!)

"They have a bunch of arms with long, sharp claws, some stuck in the ground called roots, some twisting in the air, trying to slash everything around them, called branches".

This is why Dad fought against these monsters. Not only that they broke the asphalt and destroyed the buildings, but they would have brought *ground* with them soiling everything, and the people living in the city would have gotten sick and died. Then Mom showed me pictures of trees from some old books she was keeping locked in the closet. They were frightening. They didn't have heads, and legs, and arms. Even the scariest monsters Bambi was fighting against had.

Then Mom told me that *damn* is just a word which Dad used because he was furious. (Aha, so when I am furious...).

Not long after, Dad, whose wounds were already healed, began to mention more and often that the Christmas was coming. For me that was like any other day, but for Dad it seemed it meant something special. I didn't know why. Maybe because the Event happened a week before Christmas and because, before the Event, Dad was marking the door frame with the pencil pressed against my hair.

THEOPHILUS POMP

So the Event came again. And together with the Event came the guy, with his equipment, and his helmet, and the shiny spinning balls, and the many blinking lights on the screen. Only that this time, when everything finished, it was different. The guy shook my Dad hand and said:

"Congratulations!"

Dad grabbed me with his arms and threw me toward the ceiling.

"This year we'll celebrate the Christmas together in town, in the Central Square" he said.

You could see he was happy, because of me I think he was happy. I was both happy and frightened, and I said:

"Yes!"

And I cried.

In the Christmas morning he gave me a gun and he said:

"This is to protect yourself from the city dangers. Now you are a man, you are allowed to go outside and allowed to use a gun."

I was very proud of my gun, I knew how to use it – learned that watching Bambi –, I was proud I was going outside, I told that to the Little Girl as well, and she made me promise I would share with her the *Experience of the outside* when I came back.

With the gun on my left shoulder, holding Dad's hand I went outside.

The city was amazing. I saw buildings touching the sky, roads with shiny cars, and men holding happy children by the hand – exactly like my father and I –, most of them taller than me. I felt I couldn't have had enough of everything my eyes were seeing around, and, moreover, nothing seemed to be dangerous, no *city danger* to protect myself from.

THE JESTER. 11 STRANGE STORIES

Not long after we arrived at a place where the city buildings seemed pulling themselves away to make room to a large flat area, the Central Square, big as hundreds of Yourroom, the place where Dad fought like a hero with the damn threes. The area was covered with a thick, white, cold, fluffy layer, which the children were using to jump and roll in, or to make small white balls they were throwing at each other.

"Artificial Snow" said Dad.

Is Artificial Snow something like a toy, something I can bring to Yourroom, I wanted to ask, but exactly in that moment I saw, right in the center of that place, something gigantic, green, with long arms and long sharp claws that was spitting sparks and fire toward the sky. A Tree! A tree invaded the Square to kill the children and take revenge against my father and the other men who destroyed his kin earlier in the year. To my great astonishment it seemed that nobody had noticed the danger. Hard to understand why, but neither the children playing so close to it, nor Dad, nor other Dads seem to have seen the Tree. Maybe it was invisible (like in Bambi-Against-the-Invisible-Ghost), and only I, through the superpowers of my mind, could see it.

I felt right away that everyone's lives depended on me; I understood that I had a duty to protect my fellows, and to defend the city. I took the gun from my shoulder, and I fired, again and again and again, until I emptied the magazine of explosive shells, and the tree came crushing down in pieces, burning and smoking on the white, fluffy surface.

Then Dad turn toward me, and yelled with tears in his eyes:

"It was made of plastic, idiot!"

And slapped me over the face, as hard as he could.

THEOPHILUS POMP

Then I understood what pain is (never before someone slapped me, and never after), but I didn't cry.

Since then I have never cried again, have never connected the jacks to my head to watch Bambi, and have never exchanged my thoughts with the Little Girl. Because it was then when I learned what to be hurt is, and I became a man.

But I keep asking myself a question, which I should have probably ask my father when he hit me, wondering in the same time why I didn't dare to do that, like a man who knows what hate is:

"So what it was made of plastic?!"

Corn

I don't know what I could do now. I am the Chosen One of the Uni tribe and I have no right to think about death; because I'm on the verge of becoming a master. And a master, the Corn, never thinks of its death. It leads its people on hunts, teaches them to make shelters, and impregnates them.

I see Gnoso, the priest, the poet, and the scholar of the tribe, my teacher and friend, coming towards me. I say I see him, and the thought of this trivial action cuts a painful trench through my nervous system.

"IT'S OKAY, THE TRENCH will help with draining the rainwater!"

Can, my former best friend, grins sarcastically from somewhere above and to the left of my brain. Some of my neurons have decided to test me. They retrieved the smithereens of his face from memory, recomposed it, and then projected a few dozen billion fregs into the place where I now feel Can's presence. The image is successful; the mosaic's cracks are inscrutable: Can's wolf-like eyes, the fleshy lips I've kissed so many times with pleasure – he was a friend you would have made love to anytime – and his crest of golden hair bordered by family insignia tattooed on the skull. If I were a Uni Art, I would have scanned it and reproduced it in stone.

THEOPHILUS POMP

Former best friend because it was just the two of us left, and the last step towards becoming the Chosen One had to be sprinkled with the blood of one of us. Every other step had to be sprinkled with someone's blood. In the beginning, there were many of us (the eternal rule of selection) and with each attempt, something else – bloodthirsty beasts, the force of nature, bad luck, or sheer chance – had always taken care to lessen our numbers. Until the last step, Can and I had fought together against that something else. But at the last step, it had to be one of us. It was only luck that I was the first to understand that. It was a hot night, with the moon about to be born in the tangle of the branches of a giant maundrin. We each connected one hemisphere of the brain to the chiral nightingale detector to stand watch, and we mated on the bank of the great river. Then Can fell asleep and I stayed up to keep watch. And in that paradoxical stillness, in whose spectrum you could have found the rustling of maundrin trees and giant ferns, the howling of the beasts, the vibration of the cron rock, the wheezing of the Winged One, and the distant breathing of the Uni tribe, I understood that all the other aspirants had died, only the two of us remained, and that it was up to me alone to become the Chosen One.

I cared about Can, it wasn't just a convention – though the way I now express my thoughts is a convention – so I made him die easily, quickly. I disconnected his nightingale, mine was the only bionic stream that didn't trigger the alarm, and crushed his skull with one of the boulders guarding the river. I did this in cold blood, the love act I had performed on him minutes before did not affect me; it was just a remnant of the ancestors' reproductive behavior, pleasure without the possibility of procreation (only the Corn can procreate, laying its eggs in the natal sacs of the Uni mothers). Then, for a while, I wept silently, alone, away from the tribe, as only true warriors can weep, and with tears in my eyes I snatched the radiating stone hanging on a string around Can's neck and placed it beside my own. I only wanted to keep it as a memory, but after some time the stones merged into one. It was my luck again: now the period after which my stone will die, after which its power – my power – will dwindle, is twice as long. My soul is orange with joy, I feel how the stone throbs on my chest, it seems to live a hidden and inexplicable life in itself.

———◉———

I NOW FEEL CAN'S HEART throbbing over my heart, and Gnoso approaches me holding two masterfully carved cron arrows in his hands, engraved with the chosen one's insignia.

Gnoso has his lab in the core of the Cron Mountain. None of my fellow Uni understands what Gnoso is doing in that cave in the rock; they don't understand many of his customs, words, or deeds. But they respect him. They all fear and respect him, because he protects them from diseases and heals them, creates new weapons and hunting spells for them, and leads them in rituals and in front of the gods.

I see Gnoso approaching. I don't know why the thought of this verb sense action comes to me so hauntingly; I'm guessing, or maybe something is telling me, in a language something else in me understands, what's coming next.

———◉———

THEOPHILUS POMP

"SEEING IS A LIE, AND the eyes are useless", Gnoso used to say to me back when I was just a Uni-Child-Preparing-To-Become-Aspirant.

And to prove his point he showed me an electronic eye, a prehistoric tool made of integrated junctions.

"It's better than the ones that leaven into your eye sockets," he said.

I didn't believe him. The object was too old to be able to believe Gnoso.

"This eye used to replace the living one. I'll implant it in your head, but a little different from how they used to do it in the past."

He dipped the pin at the base of the electronic sensor into a scout plurivirus culture, and then stuck it in the back of my head. Then he blindfolded me. After a while – the scout had been programmed to seek out the nerve center of vision, attacking fat and muscle cells and transforming them into neurons, altering the neuron connections and creating a new optic nerve, and dying – I began to see what was going on behind me. Gnoso had been right. The images coming through the artificial eye were much sharper, and fuller of minute details, nuances, shades, and shapes than those my own eyes were serving me with.

NOW I'M IN THE LAB in the heart of the mountain, and Gnoso is holding two cron arrows in his hands.

"Seeing is a lie and the eyes are useless", he says and sticks the arrows into my eyes.

THE JESTER. 11 STRANGE STORIES

The gesture has a force I never had guessed at Gnoso. I first hear a short pop, my eyes burst like two grapes, a warm liquid trickles down on my lips, and my brain is scratched by the harsh gnawing of the arrowheads rubbing against my eye sockets. I howl in pain and helplessness. The rock shakes, it's the chilling howl of the wounded Chosen One, I wonder how many similar howls have been recorded by the cave's sensitive walls. But I make no move, I know this is the ritual and I must endure it, I am on the verge of becoming the master of the Uni tribe, and a master should have no knowledge of what pain is. I stand frozen before the priest and wait for his words:

"As many years
As the many stars in the sky
Have passed
Since Uni has been Lord of the World.
Uni hunters
Are braver than the horned tiger,
And its mothers
Are more fruitful than the yellow bees.
The people before Uni
Live in Uni,
The powerless people before Uni
Are happy to live in the Lords of the Planet.
The deep green of the giant fern
Is no more intense than our love.
We are Uni."

The litany flows like a balm, the arrows have taken root in my eye sockets, the eyes I no longer have no longer ache, the priest's song snakes through me cutting bright trails and raising roiling waves, the blood of hundreds of Corns who took turns

THEOPHILUS POMP

laying their eggs in my ancestors' natal sacs before I was born burns my veins.

I perceive, eyeless, the glittering image of Gnoso chanting in trance:

> "Behold distant cousins
> From the constellation spread
> Like the Winged One in the sky:
> One is the Chosen One,
> One is the Winged One,
> One is the battle between them.
> Behold the mighty people of the Uni tribe:
> One is the Chosen One,
> One is the Winged One,
> One is the battle between them.
> Watch and shout
> Distant cousins,
> And mighty fellows of the Uni tribe,
> Let your cry be a million times
> Louder than the great Vulcan's scream.
> Let your cry
> Whip the planets,
> Quench the suns,
> And anger the Old Man
> Who sits behind the Universe
> And tends it.
> Hear ye distant cousins:
> May the Messenger be born,
> The one who will gather in him
> The face of Uni,
> And your face.

THE JESTER. 11 STRANGE STORIES

We are Uni.
We are Uni!"

I feel a mountain of strength growing in me. Gnoso gleams fadedly in front of me. He must be exhausted. But no, he starts talking again, this time directly to me, without incantation. His voice is soft:

"Now you will begin the hunt for the Winged One. If you win, you will be the Corn of this tribe for ten agings. If not, your body will become food for the limestone locusts, and your name will be erased from the history of Uni. It will not be found in its legends, the memory of the cron rock, my brain, or the brains of all Gnoso who will come after me.

All Gnoso who will come after me... Truly the priest, poet, and scholar of the tribe, my teacher and friend, is different. Even his procreation is strange. The thought of Gnoso's birth twists my insides, which are ready to spew vomit. He did not hatch from a master's fecund egg, but from a woman's disgusting belly and through a woman's disgusting vagina. I think I'm the only one – why me? – who knows what a woman is. Who has seen a being so named. The other Unis have only heard of it in myths.

ONE DAY I WAS A UNI child in Gnoso's laboratory cave. And from the hall of wonders, as I later called that part of the cave, sounds began to reverberate, deep and mournful, or rushing like the river's march at the springs, dark as the storm's lightning-laden clouds, spellbound like rainbows playing on the leaves created by the light breaking through the morning's dew. I walked in and saw Gnoso playing one of his ancient devices, an audio-chromatic synthesizer. He saw me too but kept playing. The music was unlike everything I had heard before. It was beautiful but it felt wrong, it felt fake, it couldn't compare to the music Gnoso produced at ceremonies playing on strings braided from maundrin bark stretched over a carnivorous elephant skin. The music he was making then was called betrayal and deceit. He was cheating the gods. I cried. I felt I wanted to kill him. Laughing as if at me, he stretched out a hand and lowered it in a mad dance across the chromatic keys of the synthesizer. And in a saraband of colors and chords, in front of me, he created his woman.

"Do you see this box?" he said "it's a memory, much denser than the cron rock (another blasphemy, nothing could be denser than the cron rock). In it, there is enclosed the genetic fabric of all the ten billion women who, together with men, populated the planet before the end of the old people".

With that memory and with the synthesizer he could recreate any of them. Then he would couple with her in the manner of the old people he mentioned. The woman would bore him a son also named Gnoso, who in turn will have a son named Gnoso, like his father, grandfather, and great-grandfather before him, like this whole line of Gnoso, as long as a strand of light linking in the longest night of the year the star of our cousins from the constellation of the Winged One to our planet, inheriting from link to link the science and customs of the tribe, the strange machinery, and the laboratory in the core of the cron rock.

Later I understood Gnoso's immense power. He is perhaps more powerful than the Corn. He has at his disposal the science (incomprehensible to others) and the potential combination of ten billion genetic patterns, those of all the women who have ever existed, plus that of the first Gnoso; whereas the Corn is nothing more than a phenotype selection in a cycle of ten agings, and the miracle that transforms the victorious Chosen One into the Corn.

GNOSO WAITED QUIETLY for my flow of thoughts to subside. He's even watched them, I believe. But I have no reason to be upset. And I'm glad I didn't think about death.

"I'm ready", I say.

A slight fluctuation in Gnoso's energy field gives me the feeling that he's smiling.

"Leave your alchemizer here. First of all, you have to defeat him without weapons. That's how it's given. He will have only the golden horn on his forehead, you the cron arrows stuck in your eyes. Then, his fur reflects radiation and you might turn yourself into dust by wanting to turn the Winged One into dust. The men who accompany you on the hunt can take their weapons. They will be useless to them anyway. You are the Chosen One."

I'm listening. I take down my weapons, my breastplate, and my shield. I stand with my torso glowing crimson in the artificial light of the cave. That's how I remember I had seen my torso many times before when I had eyes, bathed in the twilight: glowing crimson.

From outside, transmitted through channels hidden in the rock, the wail of the Uni tribe vibrates. I concentrate and try to see them. A snake gathers inside me, curls into a ball, and aims forward like a fist thrown into the bulging forehead of a grob you want to catch alive and take its milk. It circles the lab and gobbles up photons with an insatiable hunger, images: Gnoso, the fog-body creation machine, pieces of wooden hands and feet, myself, the brown cave wall, then darkness. A whole cosmos of darkness into which the Bright Snake enters and wanders, not knowing which way to turn, writhing like a real snake. The darkness bites slowly into it and extinguishes its light.

"The cron shields you", Gnoso utters; his habit to spoil with cold words, known only to him, what for me was a struggle to see beyond. "You were wrong to want to see through the rock. You must see with the rock."

Then:

"The gods are strong! The gods are just! The gods are generous!"

It's the greeting of those who go hunting. Sometimes of those who go to death.

I answer him in kind and go out. The valley stretches green with yellow strains like a lizard's skin. A group of Uni tribesmen meanders to the sacred place by the river in a funeral procession. The river trickles like an earthy spit along the valley. At the head of the line, two tall Uni with bodies painted with black stripes carry in a twisted spike of irbantine alloy a three spears-long puppet – half human-half horse – that flails its hands and hooves, writhes as if seized with rage and sings. Uni symbolically buries the one who will die in today's hunt, for no matter who it is, it is written that his body won't have rest. The puppet is Gnoso's devilish invention. I imagine a host of motors, pistons, gears, transmissions, and vibrating strings – tiny parts culled from his fantastic laboratory – wriggling in the puppet's belly, head, and limbs. I wonder if even the gods are nothing more than a Gnoso's devilish invention. If there's anything to truly believe in.

"You know, the legend says, and I didn't invent the legend" Gnoso slipped in my head and speaks "that the law that makes Gnoso's woman to always give birth to a Gnoso boy is not always law. It happens rarely, maybe every hundred of thousand years that there is something, a virus that breaks the program, and then Gnoso's woman gives birth to a girl: a being like a woman, but different. The girl's name is the Maiden. And the legend also says that once it will happen that the girl does not die immediately after birth, but grows up, and meets the Corn who impregnates her in a different way than the Uni mothers. Out of that mating, the Messenger will be born, the one who can be at the same time with us and with the cousins from the constellation

of the Winged One,
Who will gather onto himself
The face of Uni
And the face of the cousins.
We are Uni!"

"Blasphemy! May thousands of snakes lay their venom in Gnoso's eyes and their eggs in his belly! And may his bones turn to glass!" I curse with unmeasured anger.

He mocks us all. I and the other Unis who just finished burying the grotesque puppet – half human-half horse – are idiots and fools.

But I don't have too much time to waste thinking about that. The Winged One is alive and I must kill it. I'm on the verge of becoming Corn.

THEOPHILUS POMP

I sit at the foot of the cron cliff and brace my body. The rock begins to vibrate with me, now I understand what Gnoso said by seeing with the rock, the metal sucks up all the knowing and unknowing of Uni's land by the inch, and transmits it through the arrows stuck in my eyes, into my brain. I send a few tens of billions of over-excited frets into the midst of my companions and they freak out seeing me suddenly materializing among them. I am here and there at the same time; there are only my senses and the image I created that emboldens them and leads them into battle. I look at them and notice that Gnoso has planted sarozaur scales all over their bodies to protect them from the blows of the Winged One.

We stand watch, tensely, for a while, and then I see it. The Winged One flies towards us. Its outstretched wings, tense neck, and fluttering mane are as white as bones washed by a hundred ages of rain and sunburn. The horn on its forehead gleams golden: the harbinger of death. The Winged One sniffs and neighs. It sees five Unis waiting for it – the others have run away hiding in the forest – but the scent also counts and brings only four to its nostrils. It understands that one of them is a fake, a projection. It hovers above us sniffing until my men lose their patience and stretch their cryogenic bows. Their pheromones inform the Winged One of the scent of the bow's movement. Only I face its approach with steadfastness. It understands who I am. The game understands that this is the day of the hunt and that I am the one who wants to subdue him. It jumps towards me in a whirling of white mane and wings. A few arrows of frost swoop past it and turn the air behind it into great lumps of ice, that fall crashing to the valley. It rushes into my image and shatters it. Uni screams in fear, and then they figure out the trick too. Their faces spell death. And they know it. They've known since they offered to join me that my defeat, or my victory, would be based ineluctably on their blood. But they also knew that this way they would enter the legends of the tribe, that they would become Coursers of the Chosen, and that their souls would be honored by their descendants and by gods.

The air sweats and takes the color of fear. The fight that broke out in the valley reflects exactly in my mind, I see for myself what Gnoso meant when he disarmed me before the fight: a Uni discharges the alchemizer and almost immediately turns into a pile of filth. Then the Winged One rips off the heads of other Unis with its golden horn and crushes them with its hooves, one by one, not even staining its pristine fur with the blood gushing from the Unis like geysers, or with their dying screams. I feel the chill of their death pervading me, but I cannot help them, and yet some time passes before life is forever silent in them. I feel their anguish in my skin, flesh, and bones.

The Winged One is weary and covered with silvery foam. It's time to face it myself.

The radiating stone trembles on my chest, Can's heart beating above my heart. I focus and call down the lightning. One of them strikes the stone and transforms it into dust and Force. I stand at the foot of the cron cliff and weave the flock of Force, weave the net with which I will catch the giant white fish with golden horn and wings.

In the heart of the Cron Mountain Gnoso laughs, sways in a lewd dance, and sings:

"Hi, hi,

THEOPHILUS POMP

> One is the Chosen One,
> One is the Winged One,
> One is the battle between them.
> Ho, ho!"

The Winged One flies towards me. It has found me. I cast the net, catch it, and with a swing smash it against the hard metal of the rock. It falls for a moment, bewildered, then recovers, and I feel how its glowing horn tears into my stomach. I leap and as I roll through the air (I realize the wound is small; I heal it) I see the sky metamorphosing around me: a spinning red wheel, black spirals, blue rivers, brown rivers, and blue rivers again. I find myself on the ground, I get up and cast the net again.

And again...

"Seeing is a lie and the eyes are useless." What's Gnoso doing in my brain?

THE PRIEST AND SCHOLAR of the Uni tribe, my teacher, and friend felt that the electronic eye demonstration was not enough. And there followed a lot of sunsets and sunrises, seasons and passages that came and went without the light washing over my eyes. Gnoso had thrown me into the great river, into the black waters of the deep, among the spitting worms and clawed cuttlefish. I had to learn my skin to breathe and my mind to watch, to shun the venom and deadly blades of the river beasts and to gather the nourishment for my body from the poisonous mud of the river bed.

THE JESTER. 11 STRANGE STORIES

"HA, HA" BARKS GNOSO obsessively, and I understand he's laughing at me. I also understand why, that he is right, and that without his help I would have no chance of becoming Corn. I claw at my arms with my sharp nails – let the blood flow, I know the smell of blood drives it mad – and wait for the Winged One to attack again. I dodge it and clutch on its mane and neck with a leap. I mount it. The beast leaps and spins in the air like an acrobatic rat, but my hands are like the jaws of a frigid corpse and remain clenched on its neck.

I think about the ground and the ground pulls me down with a force greater than that of its great white wings. We both plunge into the river, the mud at the bottom is blinding and drowning us. The Winged One struggles to get out, but its mired wings bind it to the water that carries us calmly and carelessly toward the great Pit, where all the poisons of Uni's country are collected: radioactive waste, sulfurous acids, the miasma of decaying organisms. And as I plunge with the Winged One into the depths of the black nectar I see Gnoso squealing contentedly, rubbing his palms in the middle of his cave.

Slowly, I begin to lose myself in the burning darkness, I can feel nothing but the body of the Winged One struggling against mine and pulling me down. Darkness again, I'm a half-man-half-horse stuck in an irbantin spike, and a screaming crowd of Uni carries me towards the sacred burial place, the net woven from the threads of the Force catches me and slams me against the rock, I'm an electronic eye stuck in the back of the head of an incredulous Uni, I lift the boulder and shatter Can's skull, I am a fertile egg of Corn slipping into the blistering bag of a Uni mother, and I scatter hopelessly along the endless rope made of brains of grinning Gnosos.

Suddenly I become weightless. I soar, light breaks the dams of the great Pit and floods the blackness, I am somewhere above the surface of the river flying towards the sun, huge white wings shading Uni's land, a white spear piercing the sky.

I am, beyond life and death, the Uni Corn of my people.

And I run to spend my happiness in the peace of the jungle; I know that somewhere there, hidden in a cradle of lotrun an unseen being awaits me: the Maiden, daughter of Gnoso.

The First Contact

His name could have been Bill. He could have been called anything because he was not born on our planet. He only came, from a far far away place, and from a far far away time, to get in touch with the human civilization, to initiate what the loony scientists, UFO hunters, History Channel producers, Star Trek fans, and science fiction writers call the first contact.

He could have been a "she", or an "it" as well, but we chose to call him a "he" because of his name. However, to be honest, no one knows why his name could have been Bill.

Like all the others of his kind, Bill had a huge mimetic ability. And this without anyone looking down on him, scolding him, or calling him, with anger and envy: "Chameleon!"

"Try to disguise yourself in something familiar to the earthlings. You'll minimize the contact shock" is the approximate English translation of one of the many directives Bill received before leaving his planet.

Others were: "Everybody will offer to buy you drinks, don't drink when you are on duty", "Look for the smart ones!", "Be careful, we are on a tight travel budget", or "Stay away from Earth girls".

And it seemed that the mission was indeed a success. He congratulated himself for his ingenuity in finding a way to expose himself close to his real image, but in the most benign way, and he was already thinking of the commendations he will receive from his superiors upon returning to his home planet.

When Bill showed up on Earth, none of the humanoids was scared, shocked, or dumbfounded, nor, at the very least, they acted surprised. Everyone seemed very interested to see him, and they were having lively discussions in his presence, some of them even giving him very friendly looks. Some were slightly impolite, by pointing a finger at him, but he didn't react, it would have been stupid to spoil the success of a first-contact mission because such of a small inconvenience. Touching also happened a few times, but it was never inappropriate.

The famous human xenophobia was nowhere to be found. There were days when people were crowding to see him.

In a very short time, Bill gathered a lot of information about humans and their planet. He realized the first contact with hundreds of humanoids. In most cases, the moment was immortalized with pictures taken by the humans with a small, flat piece of equipment, pictures that, as Bill learned, the locals would call "selfies".

It seemed that they gathered enough information as well, because, as of late, the number of people coming to check on him was smaller and smaller. The excitement of seeing him was fading away. Very seldom did some lonely dude give him a quick, indifferent look. He decided it was time to return to his home planet.

But he didn't get the chance.

It was a dark, wet, cold late fall evening when someone tore down the poster and Bill died pulled apart in pieces.

Ogi's Problem

$IQ_n = \Sigma\ IQ\ /\ [(1 + \varepsilon)^n \times N_0]$

THE YEAR WAS 2072, and the world's problems seemed to have been largely solved by the global government that had been created about ten years earlier under pressure from the major corporations, which had already controlled national governments for the longest time.

Wars had ceased worldwide, global hunger had been eradicated, there were no longer rich and poor countries (since the entire globe represented a single country which, we have to admit, like any other country, had its more backward regions), all inhabitants of the Earth contributed to the general well-being according with their abilities, while their daily living was provided according with their needs, and everyone was free to choose what they wanted to do and where to live. They were free to choose their ethnic affiliation, religion, gender, and skin color.

Even pollution and global warming were on the verge of being eliminated, thanks to the discovery of practical means of controlling and using nuclear fusion, which had proven to be a clean and inexhaustible source of electricity. People moved around from here to there, for work or for leisure, with zero emissions: by electric trains, trams, trolleys, chairlifts, gondolas, or anything that could be connected to or pulled by an electric cable. For those who stubbornly insisted on owning their own means of transportation, the problem of pollution caused by the production of batteries for old-fashioned electric cars had been solved by inventing the super-elastic carbon nanotubes cable motor. The motor was actually a winch on which the extremely thin cable, about the thickness of a hair (for practical reasons, so that it could be seen by auto mechanics, and to avoid any work accidents, since the cable made of nanotubes could have been so thin to become invisible to the naked eye and so capable to leave the mechanics without fingers, limbs or even heads), and several kilometers long, was stretched to the maximum by an electric motor at a charging station. The relaxation of the cable transformed the elastic energy into rotational motion, which, through a continuously variable gearbox, was transmitted to the car's wheels, providing a range of over 1000 miles.

The airplanes were launched with huge slingshots, of course electric ones, and marine transport ships had been dismantled along with the exchange of goods; thanks to the inexhaustible energy available and to the nanotechnology, anything could be produced anywhere and as much as anybody wanted.

People seemed to be happy and were multiplying like rabbits. By 2072, they had reached 12 billion and showed no signs of wanting to stop there.

And yet, in this apparent absence of global problems, Ogi Ogi, the prime minister of the world government, convened the emergency committee of the world government in an emergency meeting. The emergency committee was made up of representatives from the regions that had formed globally, prior to the final unification, by strengthening and consolidating the traditional global spheres of influence. They were: the United States of United States and America and Mexico (which changed its name every five years, back and forth, to the United States of Mexico and the United States of America), Everything South of the United States of United States of America and Mexico, the 3A Federation (Austria, Australia, Africa), What is Left of Europe, the Scattered Union of All Islands No One Has Heard Of (which, after the assimilation of the former Great Britain, changed its name to "...No One Cares About"), the Former Empires of Asia and, last but not least, Chinada (which was actually created first and immediately flexed its muscles by building a unification bridge between Vancouver and Shanghai, across the Pacific and over countries such as Korea and Japan, which later, out of jealousy, joined the Former Empires of Asia). The names of the representatives were: Dogi Nogi, Mogi Iogi, Sogi Logi, Pogi Rogi, Fogi Togi, Gogi Vogi, Bogi Zogi. Of course, these were not their real names, but code names, which the members of the emergency committee assumed as soon as they were elected to office, so that the shame of the decisions they made as public figures would not be attached to their real names. The phonetic structure of these code names came from the fact that, for an outside observer, independent and neutral, the discussions in the emergency committee (as well as in the extended sessions of the world government in general), sounded like baby talk.

„Dear colleagues," said Ogi Ogi, „I have convened you here to give you some bad news and some good news, to make you a proposal, and to invite you to make a decision. The bad news is that, after ten years of intense and in-depth studies, the special research group founded by one of the first decisions of the new – at that time – world government has scientifically confirmed the cause of the phenomenon that has been statistically observed since the beginning of the century, which is the continuous decrease in the average IQ coefficient at the global level. What was considered a joke fifty years ago - 'the total amount of intelligence in the world is constant, only the population is increasing' - is the true truth! Moreover, there appears to be a transfer of intelligence between generations with a delay period of five years. To give you an example, if we add up the IQs of all the people who died this year and the IQs of those who will be born in five years, the two resulting numbers will be identical. No additional IQ points, none missing. It's just that in five years from now, more people will be born than they will die this year. This means that, on average, the poor babies of the future will be dumber than the old farts who are passing away now."

Ogi Ogi saw the stunned faces of the extreme emergency council members and immediately realized that his speech had become a bit careless.

„Ladies and gentlemen," he said, „in mathematical language, if, let's say, N_0 is the population of the world at the initial moment, ΣIQ is the total IQ that remains constant, n is the number of years, and ε is the annual population growth rate, which for a sufficiently small n, we can approximate as constant, then the average IQ after a number n of years, disregarding for a moment the five years delay, will be: $IQ_n = \Sigma IQ / [(1 + \varepsilon)^n \times N_0]$."

THE JESTER. 11 STRANGE STORIES

Ogi Ogi had no idea what this equation meant when he received it from the group of researchers, but a mathematics graduate who was accidentally accepted as intern by the world government managed to explain it to him somewhat, enough for him to use it as a rhetorical effect in his speech.

And it had the desired result. The seven members of the emergency committee were staring at him with their eyes popping out and their mouths agape.

„To give you an example, if the population growth rate is about 2% per year, in the next five years, the generation born in 2077 will have an average IQ about 10% lower than the generation that will die this year. Or, to put it bluntly, our generation is doing quite well (almost all members of the extreme emergency council were around 100 years old, medicine had made amazing progress too), but those born now are on average three times dumber than us.

„Dumb, but many," muttered one of the council members, unaware that the expression had already been used more than 200 years before by an obscure writer living in what is now known as What Is Left of Europe, in a treatise on deficient governance in 16th century Eastern Europe.

„Intelligence, gentlemen," pretended Ogi Ogi not to hear, „is an extremely... extremely... limited resource... and we must seriously consider how we will use it from now on."

Ogi Ogi said this last sentence slowly and forcefully, so that the members of the emergency council had no doubt that the problem of intelligence as an extremely limited resource required very serious consideration.

After a few precisely calculated seconds of silence, he continued:

THEOPHILUS POMP

„The good news is that, although they haven't yet explained the mechanism by which intelligence is stored and transmitted in the natural environment, researchers can collect and store the intelligence of deceased individuals with 90% efficiency."

There was another pause of a few seconds, during which, if they had not been eliminated by a government decision a few years ago, flies would certainly have been heard buzzing outside the soundproof, thermally insulated, and projectile-proof windows of the council chamber.

„Ladies and gentlemen, intelligence is an emergent property (the prime minister of the world government pronounced the word 'emergent' by making each 'e' as long as the faces of the members of the council) of the complexity of the synaptic pathway network. The more complex the patterns of synaptic creation are, and the more diverse the neuronal connections formed use pathways for the transmission of electrochemical signals between neurons, the higher a person's IQ. We can save 90% of a person's IQ by copying all 1000 trillion synapses."

Ogi Ogi liked huge numbers, he pronounced them with great pleasure, rolling the zeros of his mouth, whether it was about the structure of the brain or the world budget.

„At the moment of death, we transfer the IQ to a computer. A server farm the size of the government archive would be sufficient to store the intelligence of a generation, that is, in our case, of all those who will die in a year. We keep the information for a period of five years, then we copy the synaptic patterns into the brains of newborns. The transfer is complete. The even better news is that before downloading, we can combine the synaptic pathways of multiple individuals in the computer so that we can decide who and how much intelligence each person will benefit from, so we will no longer leave such a precious resource as intelligence to the mercy of a natural, random, and irrational process. The peculiarity (the six syllables of the word came out slowly, as if Ogi Ogi had savored each one, caressed and rolled each sound with his tongue with great pleasure; he had learned the word from another intern, a linguistics specialist, who had somehow ended up in the government machinery) of the process devised by researchers is that the information that emulates the structure of biological brains cannot be stored on a static memory support, but rather in RAM memory, so we will need to build special servers that will be on all the time..."

„...Energy is, thanks to Mister Rutherford, unlimited!" Ogi Ogi smiled embarrassedly as if he had to mention this unimportant drawback. Unfortunately, he had found no other way to use the word peculiarity.

„My proposal is to adopt this method of storing and transmitting IQ as soon as possible. Then we have five years to decide on what criteria to redistribute this limited resource which is the intelligence."

To Ogi Ogi's surprise, who did not expect any opposition, especially after such a rhetorical tour de force, Pogi Rogi asked to speak. Pogi Rogi was his main rival and seen by most as his successor in case the opposition won the next elections.

„Well, if intelligence is such a limited resource, can we really afford to lose 10% of it every 5 years? Didn't you say that the process found by researchers has an efficiency of only 90%? How can you propose such a foolishness, such negligence towards future generations?"

THEOPHILUS POMP

Ogi Ogi's face suddenly lit up. He had expected a much more serious opposition.

„Well, who said we're losing 10%? I only said that 90% of a person's IQ is recovered in RAM memory. That just means that the difference returns into the nature and is redistributed randomly like it is now. Nothing is lost, 90% is gained. Controlling 90% of such a precious and important resource, I think it's quite good. When have ever the governments of the world had control over 90% of the world's oil reserves?" Ogi Ogi finished to the applause of the other seven council members.

The proposal was adopted unanimously.

WHAT THE EMERGENCY council, called in an emergency meeting by the prime minister of the world government, did not anticipate when approving the proposal was the difficulty of establishing criteria for the redistribution of intelligence collected in the government servers. These were no longer scientific criteria but purely political ones. Meeting after meeting and debate after debate, in expert committees or in the plenary of the world government or parliament, they had not reached any result. Opinion polls and press campaigns had also failed miserably. There were too many differences of opinion, too many proposals, some of them downright crazy, many contradicting each other, and for absolutely all of them, even for the seemingly reasonable and common sense ones, someone had ended up finding irrefutable counter-arguments (as the linguistic intern of Ogi Ogi would say).

THE JESTER. 11 STRANGE STORIES

For example, it had been proposed that the majority of intelligence be distributed to blonde females, as a kind of historic reparation. Everyone had acknowledged the merit of the proposal, but no one could guarantee that, due to the freedom to choose sex and color and the existence of technologies that made this transformation possible, blonde females would not later become brunette males. Then someone had the idea that those who should benefit from a higher IQ were engineers, teachers, and doctors. Only that it was extremely difficult to predict the profession that a newborn would have. And even if the government had taken care to ensure that babies endowed with the corresponding IQ followed the predetermined career, most engineering, teaching, and medical positions were already occupied by artificial intelligences, and human engineers, teachers, and doctors were in technical unemployment. Opinion polls had suggested that the available intelligence should be attributed mostly to future politicians. Government and world parliament members had vehemently opposed it. If young politicians had a high IQ, then all those currently in office would be quickly replaced and none would reach the fruitful and productive age of 100 in office.

Thus, five years passed from the emergency committee of the world government decision to capture the intelligence of the deceased on electronic support. The committee met again, some of the members had changed, but Prime Minister Ogi Ogi was still in office. In the absence of a solution to the IQ redistribution problem, he proposed that the collected intelligence be kept in RAM type memories, and the generation of newborns who were supposed to receive in the coming year should only benefit from the 10% redistributed in a natural, irrational, and random way. A sacrificed generation was still a minor sacrifice compared to the future of all humanity.

It was also decided to increase the storage capacity of government servers, since they could no longer be reused every 5 years. Year after year, the solution was delayed, and the decision remained the same, until it became almost a routine.

───◉───

IT WAS THE YEAR 2097 and all the world's problems had been solved by the world government, except for one that the world government had created itself 25 years earlier. Ogi Ogi, the prime minister of the world wovernment (but different as a person from the one 25 years ago, according to the principle that people pass, code names remain) called for an emergency meeting of the world government's council in an emergency session.

„Dear all," he said, „I have called you here to give you some bad news and some good news, to make you a proposal, and to invite you to make a decision."

„I hope it's not another decision that will require more than 25 years of debate," Pogi Rogi, the prime minister's main rival (also different as a person, according to the same principle) said ironically.

„The bad news," ignored Ogi Ogi the intrerruption, „is that we have lost all the intelligence accumulated in the government's servers over the last 25 years. Someone (Ogi Ogi avoided saying who, in fact it was his nephew, a graduate of global political relations whom he had hired as a goverment intern in place of the mathematics graduate who had been transferred into educational field and who was now – of course – among those on technical unemployment), thinking it was strange that the servers were kept running at night, and to save electricity – even though the electricity was unlimited – had switched off the power to the server farms that housed the IQ of 25 generations. For those who don't know, the nasty thing (it seemed that the other intern, the linguistics graduate, shared the same fate of technical unemployment) about this intelligence is that, because of its dynamic properties, it must be stored in RAM. You turn off the light, and poof! It's gone."

The faces of the seven members of the council showed a state of profound shock. They couldn't believe it. Did this mean that they no longer had to worry about the problem that had terrorized the government, parliament, and public opinion for so many years? If there was no more intelligence, there was no need for criteria for its distribution, right?

„The good news is that if there is no more intelligence, we no longer need criteria for its distribution." Ogi Ogi continued.

„Moreover, it has been statistically proven that the generations born in the last 20 years, who have benefited from only 10% of the total intelligence coefficient of previous generations, and that distributed at random by mother nature, have had and have no problem with social integration and functioning. Moreover, the happiness index of people between 0 and 20 years old is much higher than that of all other age categories. It seems that the human race does not need intelligence to exist."

Then, after a few seconds' pause:

THEOPHILUS POMP

„My proposal is to continue recording the synaptic connections of the deceased in RAM. Then, on December 31 of each year, at 23:59:59, we press the switch, and poof! We add another brick to the happiness of future generations. I know this is a decision of great responsibility that I am asking you to make, but don't forget: that's why we are here, to take all of the whole world weight on our shoulders... Who is in favor?"

Seven hands shot up at the same time, and seven deep sighs of relief burst from the chests of the members of the world government's emergency committee.

The year was 2097, *all* the world's problems had been solved, the world's population had reached 15 billion, and people were continuing to multiply like rabbits.

Don't miss out!

Visit the website below and you can sign up to receive emails whenever Theophilus Pomp publishes a new book. There's no charge and no obligation.

https://books2read.com/r/B-A-IOUNB-QQPKD

BOOKS 2 READ

Connecting independent readers to independent writers.